W9-DAG-250

Waimea Summer

For Donald Angus
one of the very
real people of
the very real Hawaii -
The kamaaina spirit
embodied
much aloha Donald
much admiration
John

Waimea Summer

A NOVEL

by

JOHN DOMINIS HOLT

Decorations by Marcia Morse

TOPGALLANT PUBLISHING CO., LTD.
HONOLULU, HAWAII
1976

This book is for Patches

FIRST EDITION

Library of Congress Catalogue No. 75–44737
ISBN (paper) 0–914916–13–0
ISBN (cloth) 0–914916–12–2

Manufactured in the United States of America

Topgallant Publishing Co., Ltd.
845 Mission Lane
Honolulu, Hawaii 96813

At four in the morning, three days after I arrived on the Big Island to pay my first visit to Waimea, I awoke and was gripped by a sense of doom and apprehension, even before I could shake off the lingering remnants of sleep. All the things I'd heard said about Waimea being a place ridden with ghosts and black magic seemed now to be true. Before this, the excitement of being at last in this place my father had so endlessly extolled, my explorations around the once handsome house and garden, and exhaustion had successfully kept back the age-old sensitivity Hawaiians have to the world of spirits. But this morning, in my darkened room, a chilling sense of portent and unseen things being everywhere had complete hold of me. The fourposter in which I'd felt quite comfortable for three nights now seemed forbidding. The handsome quilt of the breadfruit design, which had been specially granted, felt now like a shroud.

Fluttering streaks of yellow light came from a kerosene lamp through my open door, dimly illuminating the floor. Unfamiliar odors—the smells of leather and gun metal and oil—mixed with the redolence of growing things, especially the blooms of the enormous magnolia that grew at the side of the front gate, filled my room. The air was cold up here at Waimea, such cold as I had never known in tropical Honolulu where I was born. In the great bed, I'd wound myself tightly into the thickness of two heavy quilts, or *kapa,* only to learn as I awoke that I was still chilled to the bone. Outside it was very dark, the thick darkness of a moonless night. I was afraid.

My cousin, Fred Andrews, was awake in the room across the hall. I could hear him cough and wheeze and clear his throat vigorously. I assumed he was dressing for the day when I heard the sounds of spurred boots clumping across the floor. When he poked his graying head in the doorway, it gave me great relief to say, "Good morning," to reach out from the chill of my dark room to the near presence of another human being, and know that the comforting preparations for daytime life were underway.

Fred Andrews, widowed now for the third time in the later years of his middle-age, was my father's first cousin. They had been good friends since Fred's first visit to Honolulu way back in the waning years of the Hawaiian monarchy. From the moment we met, I viewed him as an historic relic: something to be treasured and admired. Responding with understandable vanity to the hero worship of a fourteen-year-old boy, Uncle Fred (as I came to call him) invited me to spend two months of a summer vacation with him and his latest brood of children, at his home in Waimea. Although Fred owned the once-handsome house where he lived, he worked as a cowboy for a great ranch of the region. In the long-past days of his youth, his father had bred the finest horses in Hawaii and owned a profitable sheep station on the rocky slopes of Mauna Kea. The house in Waimea and scattered land were all that were left of Uncle Palani's vast holdings.

"Get up and have coffee with me, if you like, boy. The kids will sleep until later. I leave for the range at four-thirty," Fred said from my doorway.

In my dressing gown and slippers, I joined him at the kitchen table.

"Come to eat in those riggin's, boy?" Fred sneered. "It's a work day! You're in the country, boy! Ranch country!" His ice-blue eyes shone like zircons in the lamplight. "Here we get into boots and breeches when we tumble outa bed. Go put on those fancy boots your pa got you the other day in Honolulu, and get into a pair of ahina pants!"

I bolted off, leaving him to ponder the look I wore as he aired his provincial view of my garb. As I struggled into the boots, using the lamp Fred had left on the table near my door, a lithe young Hawaiian with a thin, bony face appeared, as suddenly as if from the spirit world, at the opposite entrance to my room. In the light of a kerosene lamp held close to his chest, he stood silent, his coppery skin, ebony eyes, and black beard all glistening in the flickering light.

"My horse, Julian!" I heard Fred call out loudly from the kitchen, as though he had used clairvoyance to determine the presence of the silent man in my room. "You can saddle Duke!" he shouted directly to the spot where the young man stood.

For a moment, I sat shivering, caught in the crosscurrent of Fred's loud, telepathic command and my visitor's silence. Then, as I resumed the struggle with my new boots, the bearded young Hawaiian said with an air of icy disdain: "Light da lamp nex' to you bed. You no can see if no more light!"

Within seconds, he had put down the smelly lamp he was holding, moved with seeming stealth to my bedside, and promptly lighted the one that sat on the chest near the bed. "I Julian Lono," he said in a voice weighted with sonority. "I'm da brudda-in-law of dat white peeg insigh da kitchen." He gripped one of my hands and shook it. "Joe tole me you was heah. You from Honolulu? You his ohana?"

"Yes, his cousin. I'm Mark Hull."

He ignored my need to name myself. "Dat's too bad foah you, but you treat me right, I treat you right! Okay, boy?"

I nodded and muttered a futile "Thank you for lighting the lamp," as he silently left the room.

"My horse, Julian!" Fred shouted again from the kitchen, his voice rasping with annoyance.

I finished pulling on my boots with a final spurt of effort and rushed back to Fred in the kitchen. I felt that my presence would somehow help avert the development of a "scene."

"He's gone to saddle Duke, Uncle Fred," I said, attempting to sound cheerful as I entered the room.

"Goddamned hoopau-ai!" he said, using that particularly defaming Hawaiian term for laziness. "How do *you* know he's gone to saddle Duke?"

"He heard you call. He was in my room helping me light my lamp. Before I finished dressing, I saw him pass my window on his way to the stable."

"Keep your eyes open, boy! That fella's no good! He's from Waipio Valley, and people from there are pretty primitive. Tell him to keep away from your room! He has no business being in there!"

Joe Kalama, a squat, muscular Hawaiian who was Fred's hired hand, dug into the coals of the cook stove, making a great racket as he returned an iron lid to its place atop the fire. I shivered.

"Cold, boy?"

"And how! I don't remember ever being so cold!"

"You'll get used to it in time."

"Oh, I like it! It's refreshing!"

Joe brought a tall agate coffee pot and set it at the end of the table by Fred, saying something in Hawaiian.

"He'll get used to our ways, don't you worry! It

never hurts anyone to get up early! We'll make a man out of him here!" Fred replied complacently.

A large jar of poha jam and a small platter of Saloon Pilot crackers sat on the table between us.

"Eat, boy, eat!"

I was too excited to care if I ate or not, but the martial tone of Fred's command was not to be ignored. I ate and Fred talked.

"I'm nothing more than a glorified cowboy foreman now. The ranch keeps me on. They feel some obligation to my father. He bred horses for the Stevensons—magnificent beasts—best they ever had! Now I check the paddocks for broken fences and watch for injured or sick critters. Great job, ain't it! For this, I get fifty dollars a month." His candor amazed me. During the Honolulu visit, he had cut such a grand figure, one far different from the aging, declassed handyman he was now describing. "You stay here today," he continued. "Joe and the kids will show you around. You can help with the work. There's plenty to do! We keep a few pigs and a few horses here and all the dogs you saw yesterday. We have fourteen of the bastards now! I used to keep more than thirty of 'em. My smokehouse had to be turned into a whore house, there were so many rutting bitches." We could hear Julian outside, leading Fred's horse to the kitchen porch. "Leave that black bastard out there alone!" Fred repeated, pointing to the door. "He's no good! He's the brother of my late beloved wife, Miriam—her youngest brother. She babied him and spoiled him. And Joe!" he said, "You see to it that Julian does his share of the work around here today, you hear!"

Fred rode off in the dim, mist-filled morning air, a flower lei on his hat. His mount was a beautiful animal, more Thoroughbred than cowpony, with long tapering legs, fine haunches, and a graceful curve to neck. The dogs sent up a chorus of hysterical barking. "Let Bob and Mapuana loose, will you, Joe?" Fred called back.

Julian assisted by releasing the bitch. These two were Fred's particular favorites of the brindled pack. Bob, a great beast just under the size of a full-grown Great Dane, was a darker brindled color, the result of a strong black undercoating. Mapuana, of similar color, might have been his exact twin if she were not somewhat smaller. The man, his fine horse, and the dogs soon melted into the dim moist banks of morning fog.

"We have peace now foah da day," Julian said, his dark eyes glistening, angry. "I hear him talk about me to you, boy! You believe?"

I looked at Julian for a long time and then turned away. In my heart, I knew that some aching hurt, some gnawing rancor, existed between cousin Fred and his youthful brother-in-law that nothing short of death could change.

I continued my private survey of Fred's house and discovered that, just as my father had always said, it had many rooms—all quite small, really, but giving one, when within, the feeling that the house was immense. I had looked at it from the outside the day before, and it had seemed disappointingly small, even dainty, an impression reinforced by the small window panes and the delicate panels of the doors. Years before, the old house had received a coat of dull green paint which now had turned a lichen gray. I did not then understand that, due to the coolness of the Waimea region, houses were built to be snug and compact rather than spacious and open, as were houses in warm Honolulu.

I went deliberately from room to room. The kitchen occupied a one-story wing joined to the main building by the butler's pantry, which led directly into the long, narrow breakfast room. Large bins provided storage for flour and rice; and in another pantry, arrays of dishes, those for everyday use as well as sets of fine china, were housed. A smaller pantry held a few preserves, jellies, and canned goods, as well as a supply of jars and large agateware kettles for the preservation of foods.

The mammoth wood stove was set against one expanse of wall, and at the opposite side of the room, sat a dumpy gas stove. This item was operated by fuel brought at great cost to Waimea in a large replaceable tank that now rested on a platform built in the very center of what was once Great-aunt Louise's fine rose garden. Windows at the north side of the old breakfast room looked out upon that faded garden—once meant to combine a flourish of roses with breakfast—its original effect now totally destroyed.

At the pantry end of the breakfast room stood a little quarter-sawed oak buffet. Opposite the windows on another long expanse of wall, guns of varying type and vintage had collected through time, as the waste of polyps collects to form coral reefs. Pictures, diplomas, animal pedigrees, ribbons, and framed newspaper reports of long-ago horse racing in which Uncle Palani's animals had triumphed occupied the wall space between the arsenal and the oak china closet which held additional trophies and souvenirs. A large elaborately framed lithograph of a "noted" (Fred's word) scientist on whose lap sat a hairy little creature called *Kroa, The Ape Boy*, dominated the encrusted wall. I wondered how long this macabre decoration had looked down upon the breakfasts of my Waimea relatives. Later, Fred offered a mumbled explanation that his father had brought the freakish little monster as a souvenir from Paris in the 1890's. A long oak table surrounded by chairs, all matching the buffet and china closet, stretched the length of the room.

Three steps led up from this room to a carpeted hall that opened in one direction to the parlor and in the other to the master's comfortable suite of two rooms and a verandah, its large guest room with verandah, and the stairs to the second floor on its fourth side. The parlor had served conveniently to separate the sleeping quarters of Fred's parents for many years, a subject I had often heard discussed in hushed Victorian tones by the family. The end of conjugal bliss for Louise Aylett and Palani Andrews a few years after their marriage had defined the living arrangements in the house.

Only the parlor, the dining room (now bedroom for Fred and his little brood), the oak-furnished breakfast room, and the kitchen were shared. Each of Fred's parents had a sitting room and a bedroom with dressing alcove, Great-uncle Palani having won the extra accommodation of a cozy porch which sat off his sitting room. Great-aunt Louise had a generously proportioned bathroom and the paved area under the rose arbor to serve as an outdoor retreat. The garden off the rooms occupied by Palani consisted mainly of lawn and tall trees, massive twistings of *Monstera deliciosa* and other aroideous vines growing wildly to the tall tree tops. One mild evening as we sat on the little side porch, Fred told me how his father with his guests would sit there with pistols and shoot the heads off wild turkeys, released from light wire cages.

The parlor was a tribute to Victorian England. "Mother brought the wallpaper from Paris when they went to the exposition," Fred told me when I said I had never seen any like it. It was brown, the lower half being a different pattern from the upper. Both designs were Frenchified inventions resembling oriental motifs. The pump organ, highly decorated with open carving backed with black satin, sat in one corner. In another, was a large glass case displaying stuffed birds and small animals, including the remains of two pet spider monkeys. Not even the cautious efforts of expert taxidermy, at a time when this skill must have reached its apex, had removed the morose expressions on the monkeys' faces which leered out from the confines of glass in absolute contempt of humans, one and all!

Over the etched glass of the front doors, opening directly into the parlor from the front verandah, heavy lace curtains from Louise Aylett Andrews' time had collected two generations of dust and mold. They would not survive a touch. Oil portraits which Palani had brought from England of his father and mother and several other members of his family, occupied some of the papered wall spaces. Framed and glassed "studies" in embroidery or petitpoint and three-dimensional constructions of wild flowers arranged to represent a microcosm of nature were hung at random between portraits. Except for the stuffed monkeys, these seemed the strangest objects in the room. They were totally inimical to the present.

The rooms were darkened by curtains. The velvet plush of chairs and sofas—some covered with black brocade, others with deep maroon velvet—accentuated the darkness. Over all hung the dank quietude of disuse: a splendid sanctuary for ghosts and dust.

As I was giving the stuffed spider monkeys a last glance of wonderment, I felt the presence of someone in the room; but my eyes kept their hold on the sad, accusing faces of the quiescent primates.

"Dis house," Julian said before I turned around, "dis house eez haunted."

I faced him now and saw his look of mockery. Was he taunting me, a stranger from the city, a close relative of Fred's, a half-frightened kid? Was I being challenged as a fair-skinned creature, a haole—because I *was* fair-skinned, even though I was nearly one-half Polynesian. There was an element in Julian's look and voice—in the things he'd said—that made me wonder if I would become the object of his scorn during the weeks that were to follow. His appearance in my bedroom earlier in the morning now seemed to extend beyond a show of curiosity for it could have been for no other reason than to create a mystery about himself that he had slipped so silently into the room.

"How long have you lived here?" I asked, slightly aloof.

"Ovah five yeah. After my seestah Miriam marry you uncle."

I stared at him briefly and then left the room. A chill had set into the house again, wafted in on the vibrations of Julian's words. I was anxious to escape the suddenly threatening gloom and rushed to the safety of the out-of-doors. In my confused reaction to Julian's arrival in the parlor and his terse, frightening announcement, I had developed a strong urge to breathe fresh air. The sun was shining, but the air still had some of its early morning crispness.

My eyes flashed in all directions, greedily seeking out prominent features of the surrounding countryside. Above the eucalyptus trees across the road upon which the house faced, the mauve mist-surrounded peak of Mauna Kea rose to the height of nearly fourteen thousand feet, a powerful and awesome physical presence. Behind us, in contrast to the lonely magnificence of Mauna Kea, the rounded, grassy Kohala Mountains protected Waimea from northern winds. These were friendly mountains near at hand, and as comforting as the engulfing arms of a lover's in embrace. In such a setting, the friendly spirit of Laka, patron of the hula, could very well be alive and thriving in the forests of lehua and koa. Mauna Kea and its frosted peak were the territory of the remote icy spirit of the goddess Poliahu.

Growth of tree, shrub, and other plants was most fiercely luxuriant. I had the sense that the Gods had blessed Waimea as once the God of the Old Testament had bestowed magical, extravagant beauty upon Eden.

I breathed deeply, spread my arms wide, and felt like bellowing Tarzan's call. I suppressed this euphoric impulse and stalked off to find the children. Julian's menacing words of a few moments before were dissolved in the vastness of land, sky, and within the hidden recesses of fragrant vegetation.

I found Fred's three children at play near a watering trough under a patriarchal pomelo tree, burdened now with a crop of enormous yellow fruit. They ran to greet me. We tromped across the open area back of the kitchen to go to the stables. Our amblings led to the wild goats, collected for future use as dog food by Joe and Julian before our arrival. The silent, frightened creatures were tied to stakes in the corral behind the stables. The children and I climbed the fence.

They were strange children: repressed, inchoate, and incredibly beautiful. Their skins were a golden brown, splashed at the cheeks with a russet glow. The dry cool air of Waimea gives people of the region the ruddy complexions that are distinctive in the island scene.

The skies are clear, the air is cool, crisp and clean as I ever breathed.

"What you doing?" Henry asked.

"I came to see the goats."

"We stay with you."

"Sure. Why not."

In the new boots, the tight-fitting trousers, and a long-sleeved flannel shirt, I felt quite the cowboy and feigned to be greatly at home in these open alien surroundings. Puna and Leihulu climbed to the topmost cross-bar of the fence and perched themsel-ves.

"Look da brown one, Lei. Nice one, yeah?"

"Yeah, nice one. Ass one nanny goat."

"Wahine goat?"

"Yeah, one nanny goat. Nanny goat is wahine goat," she finished in a scolding tone.

"You like to ride horse?" Henry asked me. "We ask Puppa to let us ride sometime."

"Your father said he was bringing me a special horse to ride."

"One ole plug, I bet!" Henry said with an air of knowing. He laughed.

Irked at the child's presumption that I would be a poor rider, I pulled away, opened the corral gate with an attempt to appear highly adept, and went to the goats. Henry, prompted by conditioned reflex, closed the gate.

"Poor doomed creatures," I muttered.

"What you said?" Henry asked.

"Nothing."

"Puppa say we going kill the wahine goat today," Leihulu said flatly.

"The nanny?"

"Yes!" she said happily.

Joe Kalama appeared from somewhere near the stables, carrying two empty swill buckets. "I jus' pau feed da peegs," he said, gesturing with his head in the direction of the pens. The pigs were squealing to their hearts' content, stirring the air about us with enormous gluttony.

"Are you going to kill one of the goats today?" I asked.

"Yes, da wahine one. She nice an' fat. Pretty soon Julian going come out. He da one keel da goats. Wheah da hell da buggah stay now?" he asked with a jaunty air.

Little Puna trudged up to me, took one of my hands, looked up, and with a somber face said: "We pet goats."

His nose was running so I reluctantly took from a rear pants pocket a new red handkerchief and wiped his nose. I touched his forehead and cheeks which seemed unduly warm.

"Puna has a fever," I said to Joe who loitered near, muttering things in Hawaiian.

"Feevah?" he said finally. "Aale mai keia keiki kane. E hupekole wale no. He always has a runny nose."

Julian appeared with two murderous looking knives and a steel. I noticed now that he was wearing the prevailing blue denim of the region, a pair of handsome Western-styled leather boots, and a handkerchief tied at a raffish angle around his neck—a blue and white variant of my red one, soiled now with Puna's snot. For some obscure reason I'd failed to notice earlier what Julian was wearing.

"Bring the female goat, the one the old devil tole me to slaughter today," Julian said in Hawaiian to Joe. The words were said with authority, with gravid earnestness.

Joe untethered the nanny and pulled her, bleating, through the corral gate. Julian sauntered off and with the air of a Roman praetor walked to the slaughtering block, a huge sawed-off koa tree stump near the kitchen porch.

"Dey going kill da nanny goat, da nanny goat, da nanny goat . . ." Leihulu sang out jubilantly.

The goat fought Joe's efforts all the way to drag her to the block. Julian at one point had laid down his knives and the steel and gone to help drag the bleating nanny to her place of execution.

"We kill goats every week," Henry volunteered.

"Your father told me about it yesterday."

"You folks ma don't kill goats in Honolulu." He used the collective *ma*, habitually inserted into English phrasings by modern-day Hawaiians.

"Sometimes in the country we go hunting and shoot them."

The dogs set off a loud chorus of barking as they

heard the sputterings of Julian and Joe—demoniacal Hawaiian oaths by their sound, for they spoke so rapidly I could not follow them. The nanny's bleats, the dogs' barks, the waning squeals and grunts of pigs, exploding native expletives, outdid all the modern atonal bombasts I'd heard on the radio.

Then swiftly, expertly, Julian slit the goat's throat. Joe had put his entire weight on the goat as Julian ran the sharpened blade, gleaming in the sunlight, across the animal's throat.

Already two iron cauldrons were steaming over a fire sweet with eucalyptus wood. Julian had collected vegetables—Chinese cabbage, turnips, and pumpkin—cut them up and stored them in two five-gallon cooking oil cans sitting near the fire to be boiled with the goat meat. Together they skinned the animal with a dexterity that flabbergasted my city eyes. I watched the performance in a state combining fascination and nausea: *liliha*, as the Hawaiians say.

The children danced round the slaughtered goat, holding their noses and pulling at its delicate horns and its hard black calloused feet. Henry helped by pulling back bits of hide torn loose from fascia tissue by Joe's swiftly moving knife.

"Dis da firs' time you see one goat killed?" Julian asked me.

"Killed like this," I said listlessly. "I've seen them shot at home. At Manulani on the ranges above the valley."

"*Oia no,* so it goes," he said with a smile that showed his perfect ivory teeth. He flashed the smile at Joe who returned it, saying something again as he had to Fred at breakfast which sounded as though he felt I was a creature of the city, a foreigner to these hard, exotic, far-flung rituals, and therefore to be pitied.

Joe's manners irked me even more than my stomach, which quivered threateningly. In extreme embarrassment I ran from the bloody scene and vomited behind one of the peach trees. I could hear the peals of laughter sent up around and above the half-skinned carcass of the slaughtered goat like pagan cries at a sacrifice. The air stank of warm blood and excreta.

"You dirty bunch of kuaaina kanakas!" I said, wiping my mouth with the handkerchief's end, not soiled by Puna. My words were lost under the swirls of laughter.

I went to my room and began a letter to my father, asking that a return first class ticket be sent me immediately, leaving from Hilo or Kawaihae, it didn't matter which.

The following day Puna kept to the large bed. I tried to feed him a breakfast of soft boiled egg, hardtack, and tea, which he refused. I cursed the fact there was no thermometer in the house, knowing from his flushed cheeks and heated forehead that his fever was high. The room smelled faintly of the camphor wood used in the drawers in which table linens had been kept before the handsome dining room had been converted into these sleeping quarters.

"I like orange juice! I like orange juice!" Puna supplicated. I heated the liquid of one of Joe's nondescript stews and tried to feed it to the child late in the morning, but he refused it and drowsed off into a deep sleep. Anxious to be freed from the confinement of the sickroom, I paid an exploratory visit upstairs.

The square central room or hall directly over the parlor was still equipped with a pair of quilting frames, now dismantled and standing in a corner. I had seen one used at Great-aunt Rhoda's on Maui. What caught my eye was a very large round table occupying the exact center of the room. The rose marble top was rimmed with bevelled rosewood two or three inches wide and supported on an elaborate pedestal with four feet carved like lion's paws. The table was as heavy and domineering as Great-aunt Louise or Uncle Palani must have been. It looked forbidding, mysterious, even threatening. I was to be puzzled by this until my cousin Laura, next door, told me of the mystic purpose it had served.

I tried the door to the room directly over mine downstairs. It was the only locked room in the house. Perhaps the storeroom Fred had mentioned.

The furnishings of the bedrooms at the north side of the house were intact, each four-poster stripped and covered with dust sheets. From the balcony over the front verandah, one looked down on the garden and main thoroughfare, and into the branches of the giant magnolia. The rooms flanking the opposite, south side of the house had been converted from servants' quarters into a crude laboratory in which pheasant, quail, beautifully plumaged endemic birds, and boars' heads were in various stages of being stuffed.

I was examining the remains of a little red bird with black markings, when Julian entered the room.

"Ei nei," he said, using the affectionate form of address. "Da boy . . . He cry foah oranch. Maybe we go get 'um. I know where piha loa ka alani." He made a gesture of abundance with his arms. "In da mountins, righ' behin' of us."

"I can't. I promised my uncle I'd look after Puna."

"We leave him wit Joe. I show you da beautiful place. We come back befoah he come home. Puna like my own kid. Since he was baby, he aloha me. Keia keiki kapu."

"Where are the other kids?" I asked.

"Dey ovah nex' doah. Da ah-dah cousin's house. Joe went ketch yo' hoss arready. By dis time, he saddle da buggah. We go queeck. We come back!"

We rode through Fred's paddocks along a narrow glass-clear stream and passed through an opening in the rock-walled enclosures secured by a single log. We ascended rapidly into areas grown thick with tree fern, koa, and lehua trees, a more luxuriant growth of native trees and shrubs than I had ever seen. Along the stream, sweet-smelling palapalai fern—favored for leis by old-time Hawaiians, pampered in pots by my mother in Honolulu—grew with the rampant vigor of weeds. Julian rode ahead, stopping several times to ask if I was all right.

"We don't ride often in Honolulu, but I'm okay," I said, trying to sound indifferent.

High above the stream we reached a plateau that extended some distance at the base of a small mountain.

"Heah! Heah! Look! You see da oranch?"

"What big trees they are!"

"Ole buggahs, dass why!"

"I wonder who planted them." They could have been survivors of the original seedlings left here by Vancouver's botanist.

"O Kekua Nalani paha! Our Lord in Heaven, perhaps," Julian answered.

We gathered oranges for an hour or longer, filling the sacks until they bulged like bags of onions at the vegetable markets in Honolulu. Julian climbed the high trees when the bamboo pole he had cut from a nearby stand failed to reach the clusters of full-ripe fruit hanging like glass balls on a Christmas tree.

"You like dis place?" Julian asked before we mounted.

"Very much! It's so wild!"

Birdsong, totally unfamiliar to my ears, sounded everywhere. Several times I saw tiny red forms with black markings flitting through the branches of lehua trees. Another species, chartreuse in color, claimed the same habitat.

"Those green birds," I said to Julian as he secured the sacks of oranges to our saddles, "what are they? I know the red ones."

"Green one is amakihi, red one is iiwi. Da helmets, da capes, an' da leihulu of da alii, all made from da feather of dese birds. Befoah, piha loa ka manu o na kuahiwi. Now only very few. O-o an' mamo, which have da hulu melemele, is all gone now." He paused a moment with a quizzical look. "How you know 'bout iiwi?" he asked.

"They have these birds at the Bishop Museum in Honolulu."

"They keep these birds at such a place?" he asked in Hawaiian.

"Stuffed, like Uncle Fred's. I'll take you there."

"Dass if I evah get to Honolulu. I nevah wen' down dere one time in my life," Julian said with a chuckle.

As Julian rode ahead on an old trail, freeing me from the task of guiding my mount through the tangles of uluhe fern, I indulged my peculiar bent of pondering human situations. Why had Julian said the things about Fred, and the Andrews family generally, last night? Why this anger, this hatred between the two men caught by circumstance to live in this uncomfortable relationship under the same roof? I knew something about kahunas and sorcery, even if the subject had been a forbidden one in our home. We were in contact with too many people of the older generation not to have been exposed to their talk and implications, much of which inevitably turned to kahunaism. The old caretaker, Kapihe, of our beach house at Kawela would wake up time after time in the middle of the night and come pounding at the kitchen door to arouse my father. Once I saw him grasping his throat, making hoarse inarticulate sounds. When he was able to speak he told my father he'd been attacked by ghosts. Ah Ling, the cook who was from old China, was similarly attacked. He claimed his dead Hawaiian wife's family tried to extort money from him, and when he refused to cooperate they had gone to a kahuna. Ah Ling was convinced for years before he died that he was at death's door time and again because "my wifee flamalee, he kahuna me, he hoomana me!"

Many strange things did go on in Hawaiian families where the mixture of blood and heritage divided one in two, causing people—much to their own distress—to combine both defiance and acceptance of the old beliefs. This certainly seemed true of Fred after only a few days of observing him in the context of his indigenous habitat. He chattered away in Hawaiian to Joe, expressing himself with greater ease and freedom than when he spoke to me in English; this was true, I thought, in his relations with other people. He ate the Hawaiian foods in the modern manner, using a soupspoon or his fingers, depending on what had been served; he sang the old songs of the region in such a way, you could be hard put to believe a man who looked as much like a haole as Fred produced the music. His house bore all the earmarks of being established by people of cultivated taste and imagination who had combined the influences of England and America and Hawaii in creating their home. I felt certain from the amount of accommodation and space offered and the handsome look of its furnishings that life had unfolded here at one time in a far different set of rhythms and activities than was true now, despite the absence of connubial bliss between the elder Andrews couple. Fred's way of life, the situation between him and his brother-in-law, were out of character with the house in its early years of existence, or in other homes created in part by the daughters of Judge Aylett and his lovely wife, Kamae.

The symbiotic character of Julian's and Fred's tenancy of the house seemed to me, dimly at the time, to be somehow connected with the decaying look of certain parts of the once-handsome property. The handy word, *breakdown*, had come to my mind. I was not yet acquainted with the sharply apropos and incisive French word, *déclassement*, which would have aptly described, if not explained, what had been happening to Fred and the disintegrating inherited empire. It was puzzling. It was intriguing, even strangely attractive, to see people so bitter and so angry, wearing to a threadbare state, with their tensions, the garment of their surroundings. As we approached the back entrance to Fred's paddock, I dreaded for a moment the thought of returning to the ruins. A sense of something being askew in my impulsively joining Julian to go for the oranges stole into my feelings. This was verified soon enough by Henry who met us at the stable.

"Puppa goin' be mad when he fine out."

"You shut up, Henalee!" Julian said angrily. "You brudda want o ka mea, na alani, so we go get 'um!"

Julian mumbled phrases in Hawaiian, which brought Henry to the verge of tears. Noticing the child's distress, Julian dismounted, took him by the shoulder, and said with a gentle look: "Nevah mine, Henalee. If Papa get mad, I take all da blame. You come now, I give you one big oranch! Wheah Leihulu? I give her one, too!"

I squeezed more than a dozen oranges, filling a small pitcher. After sweetening the frothy and fragrant liquid, I took it to Puna. Joe and Leihulu were sitting in the bedroom. Puna was fitfully tossing and mumbling. He half rejected the first glass but, after being adjusted on the pillows to a sitting position, finished it and then drank three more.

The argument began as we finished dinner. Julian asked me if I was going to make another pitcher of "oranch juice" for Puna.

"Orange juice? Since when has orange juice become such an important thing around here?" Fred said coldly.

"We rode into the hills today to get oranges. Puna was fussing all day for something cold to drink," I said.

"Well, I'll be forever Goddamned!" Fred growled.

"When Julian mentioned the orange grove I thought it would be a good idea to go for oranges. We are always given orange juice at home when we have colds."

Fred had turned the color of watermelon and followed Julian to the kitchen. "So you took this kid to the mountains without my permission! He doesn't know how to ride a horse! He doesn't know a damned thing about this place!" His voice had reached a shrill treble, screaming mostly in a Hawaiian I could not follow. Julian levelled his eyes a long time on Fred before launching a counterattack, using the vilest, most insulting imagery from its native source. The raging exchanges were interspersed by futile cries from Puna in the nearby room."No fight, Puppa! No fight, Uncle Julian! Pau! Pau!" Henry and Leihulu huddled on the landing.

"I'll shoot you, you son-of-a-bitch!" Fred shrieked.

"Go 'head! Shoot me! He limu pae wale 'oe!"—the Hawaiian epithet for slaves—"a piece of drifting seaweed." "You *jealous,* an' you no like him heah what I have to say 'bout you!"

"You filthy black bastard! I'll show you!" Fred raced to the bedroom for his pistol. I tried to block the doorway, but he pushed me aside like a screen door. Puna was crying hysterically, sobbing things I could not understand. The other children had clamped themselves to their father's legs.

"No, Puppa, no Puppa, no Puppa!" they wailed.

Julian stood his ground at the kitchen door, Joe Kalama beside him a silent, proud, and saddened moe pu'u, companion in death. "You kill my sistah!" Julian charged, breaking from Hawaiian into pidgin. "You kill her wit you Goddamn pilau style!" Sobbing, he went back to Hawaiian. "You are a pig, Analu! Oe waiwai koko pilau! I will shit on your grave when you die!" Julian shouted, excommunicating himself from the house forever. He had flaunted the accusation, Joe informed me later, that Fred had prayed people to death.

Fred held the pistol against his right hip. I ran into the room and stood between them. All the dogs had begun to bark.

"Get outa the way, you little bastard!"

I stood my ground, convinced that in this madhouse—in this room where *Kroa, the Ape Boy,* dominated the walls—I was going to meet my end.

"Black pig, you!" Fred screeched. "You are going to shit on my grave? Don't try your kahuna nonsense on me, or you'll know what it is to be eaten by maggots! Now, get out!"

"I go with pleasure, Analu! My heart is clean. Yours iss black!"

I went to my room, stuck the letter I'd written my father the day before into my shirt pocket, and entered the dusk-gray parlor. I sat heavily on the sofa, the back of which faced the huge glass case of stuffed creatures and stone-age artifacts. The room with its ancestral portraits darkened quickly. The house was silent except for small noises from the kitchen. The tears had already begun to stream down my cheeks, warm, and, for some reason, comforting. After a long time, Fred poked his head into the room from the stile landing, holding a lamp carefully to one side to avoid singeing his mustache.

"Thought you might be in here, boy," he said. "Come and eat."

"I'm not hungry."

"O c'mon, fella! I lost my temper a little bit. Hell, everybody does that!"

In the yellow lamplight, his pink face and the handlebar mustache, his pale-gray eyes and the bushy brows above them, had the look of a Mephistopheles I'd seen in an elaborately illustrated edition of *Faust*. I rose slowly and followed the lamp to the table.

Just before the meal was finished Fred said abruptly: "I've asked Joe to drive me to Honoka'a. I want Dr. Brown to look at Puna tonight. Will you look after the kids?"

Leihulu and Henry began to snivel. "We want to go with you, Puppa."

"That's enough, Henalee! Enough!" And then, turning to me, he said: "The part in today's shenanigans that I really don't like, so far as you are concerned, Mark, is that you are here as my guest under my protection and care. I'm not being pig-headed. Your father would never forgive me if anything happened to you during this visit to Waimea." Fred swallowed the rest of his tin mug of tea and rose full height from the table. "Let's go, Joe. It's getting late."

He went for his hat and jacket and looked in on Puna. When he came back to the kitchen, he said very gently, "You and the kids clean up for Joe tonight, will you? And stay with Puna, eh, boy? He seems to be coughing a lot." His voice began to crack.

After clearing the table and washing the dishes—Henry and Leihulu sniveling nearby—we retired to Fred's bedroom. Puna tossed and turned in the big bed, still coughing and sobbing. I helped him blow his nose, felt his neck and cheeks, and was certain his temperature had reached the danger point. I asked Henry to go for a pan of cool water and a washcloth.

"Come with me, Lei. I scay-ed go by myself."

Leihulu dutifully followed him and soon they returned with one of the old china washbowls, filled nearly to the brim with water, which Henry attempted to keep from spilling by holding high in front of him. Leihulu followed with the matching pitcher, half-filled. Tucked into her fingers, tightly grasping the handle of the big pitcher, was the washcloth. They watched to judge what I would do.

"I'm going to wipe Puna's neck and face and hands with cool water. You, Henry, help pull him over to this side of the bed."

Puna resisted, sputtered unintelligibly, and, I thought, deliriously. I jockeyed the husky, frightened, and tearful little body across the bed, wet the washcloth and began to run it lightly across his burning forehead and cheeks. Henry and Leihulu rubbed their brother's hands and begged him to lie quietly. I wiped away the streaks of tears and sweat, and the child began to relax, until he lay as still as a newborn colt in one of the Poo-kanaka paddocks.

I had been dozing in Fred's large leather easy chair when I thought I heard someone mumbling—a friend and Julian perhaps on the porch next to my bedroom. As I listened, I realized it was more like an intonation—a litany being sung—and all the sounds came from a single voice.

My body froze, my skin tingled as goose bumps formed all over. The lamp had burned so low I could barely make out the forms of the sleeping children which my eyes greedily sought. I raced to the lamp set on a table at the far side of the room and turned up the wick. For one moment the flame flickered and sputtered as though it were going out. Then—I thanked Heaven—a large yellow tongue of fire leaped to the fluted top of the glass chimney.

The sounds came from my room, black with the night: the wailing, lamenting ku-wo tones of the kanikau. I had heard them only a few times in my life: at a funeral parlor, on Maui, and, on Oahu in the country, far from town. The chant from my bedroom was the death wail.

I shut the door. I paced the room, holding my hands over my ears. The singsong lamentations were eerier in the softer tone. I let my hands fall, clenched them, and struck my thighs. Perhaps Henry knew the chanting: something to be expected at intervals in this house. If I wakened Henry the other children might be aroused. These sounds would throw Puna into delirium. Each room in the house, each item passed before my eyes, until they settled on *Kroa, the Ape Boy* and the stares of the stuffed monkeys. I fell to the floor and settled on my knees. "Oh God in Heaven," I prayed in the merest whisper, "If ever I have had cause to doubt your great goodness, your great love..."

Then footsteps sounded softly in the hall. I raised my head and stared at the doorknob. I was crying as the door opened. The tall thin frame of Julian Lono fell across the vaporous vision of my tears.

I rushed to the door and tried to strike him on the face. He caught my hands, pulled me into my bedroom, and closed the door behind us. Now I could see that his face was wan, almost ghostly; his eyes, as red as lava.

"You scared me, Julian. What is the matter with you people in this terrible house? What is happening? How is it to end?"

"Aale huhu oe ia'u, keiki. No get mad wit me, boy, please. I was praying for Puna da 'ole way. To protect from ewil spirit. Da tings I can onny say in Hawaiian."

"Yesterday you told me this house was haunted. You came into my bedroom, a complete stranger, and frightened me half to death. Tonight you looked like a devil! Why didn't you wake me before you started to chant?"

"How you going call somebody an' tell dem you going to chant? 'Smattah wit you, boy? It's one secret ting!"

Stifling the sobs that continued to come, I sat in one of the rocking chairs. "I'm leaving this place," I said. "I've already written a letter to my father."

"No be mad, boy! No go home! You no can go till Puna is pau sick! Puna need you! Henalee and Leihulu need you! Even you uncle need you! You good foah dem, I know! *I* go 'way."

"Where will you go?"

"I don't know. Kawaihae, paha? Or maybe Kona? My hoss is saddle arready. Soon as I heah da car come, I go, even if I haff to ride all night."

"But, Julian, you're the only one I . . ."

"You very differen' from mos' kids I see, boy. You have giffs from God. You are punahele, He keiki kapu oe. You stay heah wit Puna, ma. You stay wit you uncle. Maybe you change his life. He need you, dass why he ax you foah come back heah wit him.

Errybody in dis town is scared of him. You teach chirren to be smaht like you. You teach Puna how for read. I come back, see you an' Puna sometime, an' I write lettah to you. Dat way you know wheah I stay, an' you write to me. Okay, boy?" I nodded. "Das da way! I know you can take dis place. Not one time in my life I see one keed like you. Some day, you know what I mean!"

Sometime later, Fred and a young Dr. Okamura arrived. While Puna was being looked at, Fred explained quickly that the family physician was absent and he had been directed to look up "this young Jap who's just come back from medical school. I hope he can do the job. I would have picked up an African witch doctor or any one else."

"He's a full-fledged M.D.?"

"My God, I hope so! Talks like a doctor. Looks like he's just a kid off the plantation!"

The doctor said Puna was in the first stages of pneumonia, and strongly advised moving him in the morning to the hospital at Honoka'a.

Fred resisted. "We have no family there. It would be impossible to drive down and back every day. I can't take any more time off. I've just had a month's vacation—two weeks of which I wasted in that useless, noisy, smelly town they call a capital. You see my point, Doctor?"

"Mr. Andrews, pneumonia is notting to fool with. He'll need a lotta care," the doctor said with an authority that belied his youthful look and occasionally incorrect English. "There is several type of pneumonia. Procedure now is to determine through laboratory tes's what variety you're up agains', an' give treatment accordingly with serums."

"I lost my late wife due to pneumonia, and several of my children. *They* didn't have to have laboratory tests and high falutin' serums! Even so, that boy is not to leave this place!"

"I'll stay with da child," the doctor said, "but in order to treat him here, there's a lot to be done."

He started giving orders with the implicit threat that he would leave in a minute, if not obeyed. The disease was "in a high degree of contagion." Puna could not be allowed to stay in the same room with others. My bedroom was spotted as the logical one to serve as hospital. Beds were moved, bedding transferred from one four-poster to another, and lamps lighted in the big room I was now to occupy—the master bedroom of old Uncle Palani's suite.

The child raged and struggled, realizing that a stranger had come to care for him. "I no like move! I no like move! Puppa! Puppa! Puppa!" Dr. Okamura patiently used his not-much-tried bedside manner to comfort the child once his bed was freshly made and pillows stacked high to keep him comfortable.

Henry and Leihulu wandered sleepily about, wrapped in their respective kapa. I was directed to make a paste and smear squares of "Mother's old scraps of linen sheeting that had been preserved for emergencies," to spread over Puna's pain-ridden lungs. Joe was to go upstairs for the linen. He asked me quietly to accompany him. No one wanted to go upstairs at night alone. There was the locked "storeroom" and that great round table in the quilting room with its pink marble top and lion claw feet. We started off, each with a lamp.

Fred called out: "Where are *you* going, boy?"

"With Joe. I'll hold the lamp while he gets the sheets." I sped down the hall.

Joe led the way. The old stairway squeaked, stripped of its carpeting.

"No scay-ah, boy, no scay-ah?" Joe whispered hoarsely.

I followed close behind, wanting to take hold of his shirt or one of his belt loops. "I came up here for the first time, today. It's quite interesting," I said to summon confidence and probably to tell any lurking ghosts that I already knew their habitat.

In the quilting room, flickers of lamp light fell on the cold marble surface of the table. I imagined seeing indistinct nineteenth-century figures sitting around it and quickly turned away. Our shadows fell across the empty walls like bits of fog passing through a tree fern glade. The smell of arsenic and formaldehyde overlaid the flower perfumes that possessed the rooms downstairs.

In the second bedroom on the north side, we found the camphor chests. Joe recklessly pulled out two or three sheets, clutched them into a lump, and muttered, "C'mon, boy, less beat it outa heah! Diss place give me goosepimple, anu e keia ke 'ena!"

"This is quite an old house," Dr. Okamura said, as we sat later drinking tea.

"It's about sixty years old," said Fred.

The doctor lighted a cigarette. "Were your folks tied in with the Stevensons?"

"No," Fred said flatly. "My father sold horses to the Stevensons."

"There's a lotta history connected to diss area. Waimea is a famous place," the doctor said, paused, then added, "Maybe I can learn a few tings while I'm here."

"Maybe," Fred said, sending a look of annoyance in my direction. I had been brought up to know it was a crime, in the thinking of Fred's generation, to be *niele*—nosy, especially about the past.

By joint effort the three of us, like clumsy fishermen laying a net, made up the huge four-poster which I was now to occupy.

"Here, boy," Fred said, "tuck that sheet tightly under the mattress. Watch the young doc! He's an expert!"

"I worked for a family in Boston the first year I was at Harvard Medical School," the doctor said.

"You hear that, boy! Harvard Medical School!" Fred yipped. "And worked for his keep, too. No wonder you Japanese are getting ahead so fast!" he concluded, sending an unctuous look at Dr. Okamura who appeared pleased by the compliment.

"I'll start preparing the poultices. Will you help me, boy?" the doctor said after the last pillow had been stuffed into its embroidered and knitted lace-trimmed linen case. The room smelled deliciously of camphor mixed with the perfume of the many blooms that covered the magnolia and pak lan trees and the shrubs of kiss-me-quick now massively covered with blossoms.

The next morning, I became the family cook.

"What in the name of hell are we going to feed that fella?" Fred had squeaked. "I can't boil an egg. Oh, I can boil a piece of beef out on the range!"

"Let me try," I offered. "I can make a pretty good omelet."

"But what about other meals?" he wailed.

"I can make Swiss steak, pot roast, and chicken fricassee."

"You can! Why the hell didn't you say so in the first place?" Fred shrieked.

"I can even make hot cakes and muffins."

"Too Goddamned many eggs. But no, my boy, no, no! Use all you like! My God, it's been months since we've had hot cakes around here!"

"The only thing that worries me is the wood stove."

"Joe will teach you, won't you, Joe? He can get all the wood you need. And when you bake, use that son-of-a-bitch of a gas stove. It's much easier, or so my late-lamented wife always told me."

Dr. Okamura slept little. Puna fell into a long delirium in the early morning hours of Thursday—almost a week to the hour since we had taken passage from Honolulu. In the early evening the child's affliction began to reach its peak. Fred sat in the dim light of my new quarters. About eleven, the sweat began to pour down Puna's brow and neck. After sponging the child for a time, the doctor came to the door to announce with quiet triumph: "It's all right, Mr. Andrews! It's all over! Your boy has pass da crisis! Plenny of res' an' food, and in a week you won't know him!"

"Oh, God in Heaven!" Fred exclaimed his relief.

Like the bird calls in the forests of Puukapu, the whistle of the gentler of the winds that blew across the wide green landscape, like the fragrance of the air, the fragile grace of Julian's slack key guitar playing, or the steady rhythmic hoof beats of Fred's horse Duke, the doctor's words had filled the pioneer room. The vigil was over.

Fred bawled helplessly in the rocking chair.

"I'm so happy, Uncle Fred."

"Then weep, boy, weep! Look at what a shameful old woman I've turned into with my waterfall of tears. The heart is a tender thing. It bruises easily." He spoke in Hawaiian.

The next day, before he left Waimea, Dr. Okamura and I walked in the field behind the Punohu house, taking the same path Julian and I had followed several days before on the trip to gather "oranches."

We stopped and took seats on two flat-topped rocks after we were over the stream.

"You're very different from you cousins here," the doctor said.

"How do you mean?"

"Da way you talk, da way you ack—in other ways, I suppose," he answered, pulling at a stem of grass, one end of which was covered with a brush of pink seeds.

"There are nine in our family. I'm the second eldest," I said.

"There are eight in my family. Three died, or there would be eleven," he said.

"Too bad," I said.

The doctor breathed deeply and swept his gaze over the landscape. "All you people from da ole families are very much alike. You are funny kine—a mixture of kineness an' indifference—sophistication an' ignorance. I'd like to see you go to a good Eastern college, Mark! You have da makings!"

"Of what?" I asked, pleased.

"Of being somebody—a leader. Have you thought what you want to do when you grow up?"

"Some."

"When I was eleven, I decided definitely to be a doctor," he said. "One of my sisters died at home of blood poisoning. I felt so helpless. It was pretty terrible to see her turn cyanotic. Why don't you plan on going to medical school?"

"Maybe I will!" I said.

"If you choose Harvard, I'll write a letter of recommendation."

"That would be terrific!"

"Don't let people hole you back, Markie! I've seen a number of young people from da kamaaina families on diss island since I came home. They're all going to seed. In Japan an' China aristocratic families survive centuries in da same province, da same village, da same houses. It's true in Boston, too, an' da ole families in New York. People here rot away too soon!"

The doctor looked at the sky and glanced at his watch. "When your uncle comes home, we're going over next door to ask your cousins to keep Puna for a week or ten days. He needs consistent care."

We followed the stream until we reached the path where the goats were tethered. The remaining billy, fastened to his stake, bleated loudly, his yellow eyes fixed on us in an accusing stare.

When we reached Great-uncle Palani's porch, the doctor let his hands fall on the railing and stood very still. "Oddly enough, I've felt here, for da first time in my life, what it's like to be rooted in Hawaii—part of its history. You know what I mean, Mark?" He was smiling now.

"I don't know, Doctor. Some of this is too deep for me," I said, and began to move away.

Just before I disappeared around the water tank, he yelled, "Goin'a miss your cooking, Mark!"

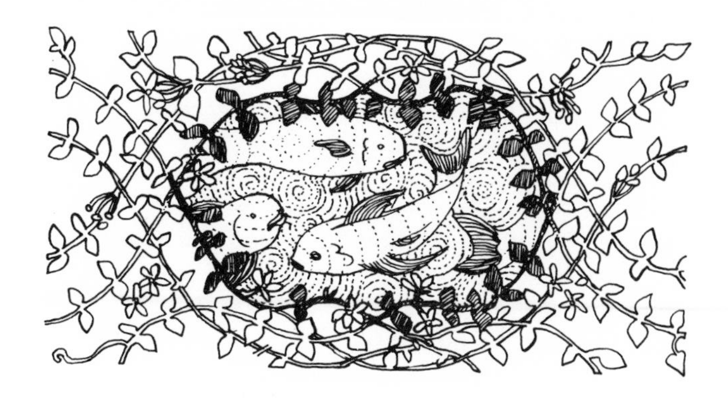

I followed Fred and the doctor next door, happy to be on the way finally to meet my cousins, the "talkative" Georgie and his elderly sisters.

Their spacious one-story house, newer than Fred's and freshly painted an off-white, was set far back from the road on a plot of land half the size of his. The driveway, bordered by generous, well-proportioned beds of shrubs and flowering annuals, all meticulously groomed, made in front of the house a grassy circle in the center of which was a small stone-edged pool abounding with carp. This was a lovely place, with a freshness, an openness, a kind of sanity I had not experienced for the past long week.

My cousins were gathered in the large, airy, spotlessly clean kitchen near the wood cook-stove, roasting a chicken which had lost a cockfight and been presented to them that morning by the Filipino gardener.

Laura, the younger sister, was tiny, tense, and fragile-looking. Her skin was pale-gray and spotted like a gecko's. "What a terrible ordeal you've been through," she said.

"This is our cousin, Mark, from Honolulu. He's

Cousin Mark's son. You remember his father—he's been here several times."

Georgie, undersized and dark, wearing a hat, occupied a rocking chair. Between his knees, he held a stick at a slant, one end of which scraped the shiny, much-painted floor as he rocked. Fred glanced at him sternly, but kept his tongue. Georgie continued rocking.

"I've come to ask a great favor of you," Fred said, clearing his throat.

The "girls" exchanged glances. Georgie let up for a moment.

"You see," Dr. Okamura said, "it's important that da child get all da res' he can get. I wanna take him back to Honokaa with me, but your uncle don't agree. He can't stay at da place nex' door!"

"I thought I'd ask you girls," Fred broke in, "if you could take care of Puna for a week or ten days."

"I suppose we could," Louise glanced at her sister and young brother. "Of course I'm away all day at the office. The job would fall on Laura, and, as you know, she's not strong."

"I'm not so weak I couldn't take care of Puna," Laura asserted with a downcast look. After a few seconds she raised her delicate head and, with the determined look assumed on occasion by fragile people, she said softly: "Of course there can be no interference of any sort from next door, Uncle Fred."

Georgie threw down his stick and left through the back door.

"I hope the boy is made to understand this," Louise said.

"He'll understand! I'll tell him," Fred said nervously, resolutely. "Shall I bring over bedding?"

"No. We have everything here," Laura said curtly.

"How about all those oranges?" the doctor said.

"No! I'll send to the store for some real mainland

oranges. Those damned things from the mountains are tasteless, ko'e ko'e!" Fred announced.

"I fine them delicious," the doctor protested. "Puna's been having the juice."

"If you don't mind, Doctor," Fred persisted. I had heard him order Joe to feed them to the pigs.

With all his dehydrated little body, Puna resisted being taken next door. He muttered over and over in a faint monotone: "I no like. I no like."

"Do you want Markie to go over and stay with you?" Fred asked.

Oh God, I thought, not really! But I nodded a *yes* reluctantly. Puna stopped whimpering.

"I appreciate diss very much, Markie," Dr. Okamura said.

"I, too!" Fred echoed, struck suddenly with a need to register his own gratitude. "Boy, I sure will miss your breakfast cooking!"

"Shouldn't someone let them know I'm coming?" I asked, apprehensively.

The idea of my playing kahu to the sick child in my cousins' house made them as nervous as me. But in the true Aylett spirit, they efficiently, daintily, and thoroughly readied the bedroom for us.

"I think he'll be very comfortable," Laura said, the taut grayish skin of her face wrinkling into a smile as she patted pillows and pulled down covers amassed atop a smallish four-poster of beautifully grained koa wood. "And you, Mark," Laura gestured with her head, "You can have the single bed we brought in."

The doctor brought a thermometer, a bedpan, and a small supply of codeine. "Da main ting," he said with a raised voice, "is to see to it he has plenny of res' an' plenny to eat as soon as he wants to take solid food again."

"That's one thing all the Andrews can do—feed people!" Louise said, her eyes lighting up, her pinkish face suddenly quite pretty. "Georgie sleeps in the room next to this one. We're all close at hand, in case we're needed."

Georgie was at the bedroom door, his hat still planted squarely on his head. "How long Puna going to stay wit us?" he asked.

He was at least fifteen years younger than Louise and spoke island pidgin. Fred and his nieces were tuned to the Englishified speech used by the older generation to keep class distinctions intact. If Hawaiian was spoken, the highly allusive and metaphoric usage of the alii was attempted.

Now Dr. Okamura was leaving. I felt a hollowness at the pit of my stomach and imagined briefly—but with fright—that I would be swallowed into the life pattern of my Waimea cousins and become forever a part of their world, at once so beautiful and so harsh.

Puna fell asleep as dusk came, giving me a chance to dash next door to gather up my things. Joe was washing dishes, and the two children sat restlessly and idly at the kitchen table.

"Where's Uncle Fred?" I asked.

"He up-stay-ah, in his small room," Joe answered.

"His what?"

"He get one small room up-stay-ah," Joe repeated.

"Puppa praying upstairs," Henry said.

I rushed to my room and quickly gathered my things, groping in the semi-darkness rather than taking the time to light the lamp. I was sure it was Fred's heavy boots that clumped on the floor above me. My belongings bundled into a lump, I clutched them protectively and hurried into the hall landing. Fred was standing at the top, holding a lighted candle. He came down, measuring each step, his eyes red, glistening in the candlelight.

"There are evil forces at work! Evil powers surround this house!" His voice was strained and unreal; his eyes, languorous yet animated.

"I came for my clothes," I said weakly.

He stared at me, oblivious. "I told you he was no good! He has left his evil in this house!"

"I have to go, Uncle Fred! They're waiting dinner for me next door!"

"Watch your little cousin, boy! Watch him! If he chokes in the night come for me!"

I said a hurried *yes* and cut through the hedge under the pak lan trees. As I struggled through the thicket of Hilo Beauty covered with velvety purple blooms, a dark figure leaped in front of me. I yelled in startled surprise. When I came into the Punohu garden I heard laughter. It was Georgie.

"You tink you bettah den us because you come from Honolulu! You talk smart—you ack smart! Jess like one haole! Up heah you bettah watch you step! I see you wit Julian all the time. I seen you guys! You know Julian is one da kine?" Georgie said mockingly close to my ear.

I clutched my rumpled burden and hurried toward the house. Above the roof to the blackening mountains beyond, thick dark streaky splotches of clouds like India ink wash drawings formed. The wind was blowing wild again, swaying perilously the great trees. The "thing" appeared first a small flame and then, as it approached, an orb. I had heard it described so many times by Hawaiians: the *akualele,* the flying god, an evil spirit sent out to find victims. It circled the Punohu house, then Fred's, and then streaked off, leaving a long coruscant trail behind. I stood frozen in my path, shaking.

"What you see?" Georgie taunted. "One ghos'?"

"Get away from me, you lousy little hick!" I said, and raced into his house.

"Is something wrong?" Louise asked me at dinner.

"I'm cold," I said.

"It's a chilly night and windy," Laura said, her eyes half-closed.

"Markie seen one ghos'," Georgie said with a snicker.

"Like hell I did," I replied irritably.

"Don't talk like that, Georgie. You'll invite them into the house," Louise said firmly.

"Eat, Mark! Eat!" Laura said, her face animated. "You are safe in this house."

She shivered.

"You're cold, Laura," Louise proffered. "Put more wood in the stove, George. Get the fire going again. Wait! Let me take out the bread pudding first!"

"Strange things surround this house. Someone is trying to tell me something," Laura said in the quavering voice of an old woman. "Take me into the parlor, Louise dear."

From the parlor, I could hear Louise saying: "Not tonight, Laura! I don't want Mark to tell his family."

"I. . . can't."

Puna awakened, but fell asleep again when I went to him.

Georgie and I cleaned up. I said nothing as we worked. Georgie cast pleading glances in my direction and finally said, "I didn't mean to make you scay-ed, Markie, I was only fooling."

"I'm worried about Puna," I said. "I wouldn't have been scared, if I was okay."

Later that evening we all sat before the fire in the smaller of the two parlors. Laura rocked with monotonous precision in an ancient chair that squeaked slightly. Louise was ensconced in a large Morris chair covered with black leather. Georgie and I were stretched out on the hooked rug, snuggled against large colorful pillows.

"How many in your family, Mark?" Louise asked.

"Five girls and four boys. Amelia is two years older than I." I felt like saying she once saw an akualele.

"Your mother is from Kauai, isn't she?"

"No. She's from Maui." A place absolutely ridden with spirits, I thought.

"She was a very beautiful woman. I remember seeing her once when she came home from school on the Mainland. I met her at a party at the Greshams' place on Beretania Street. I was a schoolgirl then. Agnes took your breath away, she was so beautiful—great brown eyes and creamy skin, and so stylish!"

"She's still beautiful," I said mechanically. My eyes were fixed on Laura who rocked in her squeaky chair. She seemed to be in a trance.

"Your father is a handsome man. Like all the Hulls."

Laura began, as though she were crying and trying to speak through her tears. It was difficult to make out her words.

Louise got up abruptly. "It's time you boys were in bed! C'mon, up with you!"

"She's trying to come back. She wants to speak . . . speak . . . to . . . " Laura wailed.

I scooted off, Georgie right at my heels.

"Aw shit!" he said once we were inside my room. "She always get like dat wen dere's trouble!"

Puna had a good day. Fred came over before dawn, tapping on Georgie's window to be let in. After the day's ride, he came again and stayed until the child wanted to sleep. Fred was not asked to dine.

"We have not been friendly with Uncle for some years now," Louise began with a stern look. "It's only because it's the humane thing to do that we agreed to take Puna."

"Arrogance and selfishness," Laura muttered.

"And cruelty," Louise added.

"We know how he treated his wives. He was ruthless. They came to us often, saying things we would not dare repeat!"

"Uncle Fred grew up with Hawaiians. He grew up wanting nothing more than to be a cowboy. Our grandfather did not interfere. Our grandmother was not allowed to. Grandpa wanted Fred to grow up 'a man'! He did, all right!"

"He could not keep his hands off a woman. He is notorious in Waimea."

"He would go off for weeks at a time with the paniolos—to Waipio, to Keeaumoku, to Kawaihae."

"It got so, Mother told us, he would hardly speak English."

"He first married Nancy Landsdale—of the Hilo family—to please his mother. He horsewhipped her in a fit of jealousy. She ran away with one of her women, the baby, and his nurse. They rode all night. Fred chased them," Laura said.

"He carried his bull whip! He would have killed her. His three other wives were all Hawaiian women, sweet enough, and kind, but commoners—country girls. He made slaves of them all! His last wife, as you know, was Miriam Lono, Julian's sister!"

"Is it any wonder they all died? He had them all scared to death. His jealousy was bestial," Laura added.

"He was jealous of the love Miriam had for Julian. They were the only two left from a family of twelve wiped out in the flu of 1920. She was a beautiful girl, much younger than Uncle!"

"When did he start that kahuna stuff?"

"Oh you know about that?" Laura said.

"Julian told me."

"Well he should know! He's one, too."

"Uncle learned all that from the paniolos, the old prayers and chants. He's been steeped in it since he was a boy! He doesn't know himself how deeply."

"You might say we come by our belief in spirits from our grandparents. That big marble table in the quilting room was used for seances. Grandpa converted grandmother. A medium lived with them for a time. Later Aunt Millie conducted the seances. She was a born medium, they used to say."

"She died young," I said.

"She was prayed to death by an old kahuna her husband had hired."

"Because he was jealous of her and wanted her money! That's what Mother always said."

"Uncle Fred has a room upstairs," Georgie said, speaking for the first time.

"Never mind, George!" Laura warned.

"He keeps akuas in dat room—two or tree stones he foun' in da fores' up Mauna Kea!"

"I told you, George, to be quiet!"

"Why does he do that?" I asked, soaked through suddenly with a new fear.

"I said, be quiet, George! Be quiet or go to your room!" Louise ordered with atypical volume.

I slept fitfully that night, dreaming of strange woodlands and stone platforms. In one dream I was a midshipman with Captain Cook. I came face to face with young Kamehameha who was studying one of the ship's cannon. He made a lunge for my throat. I awoke and saw a mask hovering over me. I yelled. Then the apparition began to laugh. I threw off my covers and leaped for Georgie's face. He ran back to his room through the hallway. I followed, pounding him on the back. He did not stop laughing. Then abruptly he began to cry. "Nough! Nough! I call my seestahs if you no stop!"

I left the room quickly. I could hear Georgie sputtering, "You Goddamned pilau haole! You Goddamned okole hi. . ." His sisters had not been aroused.

I lay awake, plotting an escape from Waimea. Spirits did not thrive in my world of bright lights, clanging streetcars, and modern plumbing, where scientific education continually refuted the lore which still clung, like coral clusters on reefs, at the outer edges of memory. Mine was not Fred's world, nor Julian's, who reminded me at times of a stately bearded Hawaiian with a gaunt John Brown face and overalls, who came occasionally to plant rare native flora in my mother's garden. Nor was mine the world of Joe Kalama who, from our first meeting had displayed a strong distaste for me and, with a limited number of words, had made it known that I was not welcome at his work. He would greet me with a grunt when I appeared to watch and fall into that vaultlike silence Hawaiians practice to perfection.

On the fifth day of Puna's convalescence, Dr. Okamura and his wife drove up. Georgie and I had been currying the horses; Georgie telling me of the time Fred had roped a boar that had killed his favorite hunting dog, strung it to a branch, ripped open its belly, then eased it down as it began to gouge out its own insides with its tusks. Georgie was an expert teller of Waimea tales.

I was overjoyed to see the doctor and meet his pretty, red-haired haole wife, Moira.

"So you're Mark," she said with a warm smile. "Kenneth has told me a lot about you."

I hoped my smile was as warm as hers.

The doctor was pleased with Puna's recovery and commended Laura, who seemed to take his blandishments noncommittally. The doctor and I walked around the Punohu property while his wife was being entertained.

"Is something wrong, Mark? You've lost a little weight. Of course, that won't hurt you," the doctor said.

"I'm a little dazed. I've heard some pretty strange things," I said. The doctor kept silent. "These people here all believe in spirits."

"I've heard about Hawaiian ghosts all my life, haven't you?"

"Yes, but not the way they talk about it here. My cousin goes into a trance. It makes my blood run cold."

"Are you frightened by all this, Markie? Do you want to go home?"

I hesitated.

"Sometimes tings affect us in such a way we don't know dey are doing us harm. You're a city boy."

"I saw a fire ball the other night. An akualele," I said with much relief. It was out at last!

"Waipio people always use to talk of seeing them. Must have been pretty scary!"

"My sister saw one once in Honolulu. It fell on a Hawaiian neighbor's house, and shortly after a baby died."

"Hawaiian people have enough trouble. It's too bad dey let themselves be influenced by this stuff from da olden times. I seen people from Waipio die for no apparent reason. It's not easy to change peoples' mines, especially if there is hunrreds of years of tradition and belief. In Japan dey all believe in ghosts. Life is full of mysteries," he said, bending to examine a flower.

"Please don't mention this to anyone, Doctor. You're the only one I've told."

"Do you want to leave, Mark?"

"I haven't done any of the things I came here to do—like riding or hunting. I want to see Waipio Valley. They say it is so beautiful!"

"Thass as good a reason as any," he said and turned back. "You're a brave boy, Mark."

Fred poked his head out the kitchen door, his handlebar mustache silvery white against his baby-pink face. "It's good to see you, Doc! How's my boy doing?"

"Jus' fine! He's coming along all right!"

After ten days, Puna's recovery was complete. The child had been on his feet for at least two days, but we wrapped him carefully in a blanket and Fred carried him home in his arms as a celebration.

"Come back and see us, Markie," Louise had said as we were leaving. "Anytime you like," Laura joined in. "I walk over wit you guys," Georgie announced.

I roasted and stuffed a turkey and served it with the pickled peaches that Hanford Andrew's round, blonde Swedish wife Gerta had put up the year before. Joe brought in Chinese peas, sweet potatoes, and crisp heads of iceberg lettuce. For the first time, I heard the laughter of the children fill the house.

"You cook like the old folks, Markie. This is as good as though my mother were here instructing Sing Wo and his helpers every step of the way. It's enough to spoil a man for life!"

"I'll cook Swiss steak tomorrow."

"That's wonderful! Can you make mock duck?"

"I could try."

"You're the boss of this kitchen now."

The mock duck and roasted joints, popovers and coconut cakes that found a place at Aunt Rhoda's table, or the piquant concoctions dreamed up by Aunt Emily's Kenji, or the elaborate fare that had graced my grandmother's table during the abundant days when Manulani ranch provided pheasant, guinea fowl, capons, and choice cuts of beef to the Hulls living in Honolulu, were nothing I could equal. But I cooked massive amounts of food. Joe Kalama felled old trees, collected timber from the woodland back of Fred's house, and stacked cords of wood for us. Gerta Andrews instructed me in making custard and pumpkin pies, German chocolate cake, and Swedish meat balls, and something she called tamale pie. Laura and Louise taught me to use the ancient iron gem pans to make popovers and extra large cupcakes ("Uncle Fred likes them that way") and to roast the pheasant and wild turkey that appeared regularly in the larder all summer. We roasted suckling pig and racks of lamb and prepared thick cuts of beef in huge quantities. The children put on weight, and Fred declared he'd have to go on a diet if he continued to ride the range. I found my belt could be a notch or two tighter.

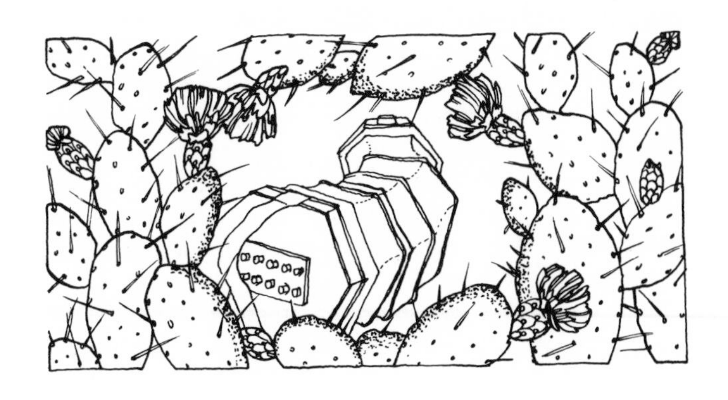

Fred brought the decanter of okolehao and his concertina to Uncle Palani's porch and talked and sang and drank until dark, the children at his feet. In the spirit of his Polynesian forebears, Fred entered into the full enjoyment of his happiness. Little Puna adoringly watched his father's fingers move on the keyboard, trying to make out how the little object produced its sounds. Finally Fred put down the "squeeze box," looked out across the lawn to the great tree tops, and said:

"I'm going to give a luau to celebrate Puna's fifth birthday! Yes, a luau! It's been a long time since this house has offered hospitality," he said in his excited soprano.

The children squirmed.

"Who going cook da pig, Puppa?"

"Who's going to do *what*, Henalee?"

"Who *is* going to cook *tha* pig?"

"Joe can do it. I can help. Mark, too! Hell, there's all kinds of specimens round here just waiting to have a good time who'd be glad to help!" Fred fell silent as though questioning the sanity of his plan. Then he spoke again; his eyes, moistened; his voice, calm and affectionate. "I know just the woman—Lepeka Lovelace! Remember, Mark, that good-looking woman in the riding party the day we arrived?"

"I can't say that I do."

"C'mon, boy! She's not so young, but she's still a beauty! The one with the greenish eyes and light brown hair? Wearing a pua makahala lei on the top of her hair!"

I recalled with some excitement a strikingly handsome, smiling woman on her horse, wearing an orange silk pa'u and a flowing cape of black satin.

"She's a half-white from an old Kohala family. She was cooped-up most of her life, taking care of her parents. She lives with a sister now, out toward Pookanaka. I had a drink with them just the other day. She used to be very religious. The other day she seemed quite peppy!"

"What about Louise and Laura?"

"Those washouts? I think they'd faint if they had to prepare guts and blood to make loko. We'll ride out and look for pigs!"

"Wonderful!"

"I'll send a horse home so you'll get used to being in the saddle."

"I do ride!"

"This is rough country."

The following day he rode in with Lemonade, an animal that Queen Victoria might have ridden safely at the Golden Jubilee. Lemonade would not do hijinks with a soft, overweight boy from the city.

"You ride English-style," Fred said as I walked and trotted on the driveway and lawn.

"At the riding academy they have only English saddles."

"Riding academy!" Fred grunted. "So you want to try another horse?" He told Joe in Hawaiian to saddle Black Beauty. "This is my old saddle horse, getting a bit old but still a wonderful mount! He's beautifully broken to bit, so you keep your hands quiet, you hear?"

"Puppa! I like ride, too!" Henry said.

"An' me too!" Leihulu echoed.

"An' me, Puppa! An' me!" Puna pleaded.

"All right! You kids take turns riding Lemonade, but don't you get too sweated up, Puna!"

In a moment, Henry had worked the old horse into spirited motion.

"He's a natural!" Fred said with an admiring look. "Make a damned good cowboy someday!"

Black Beauty was indeed black—a gelding, sleek with fat, a fiery charger compared to Lemonade. The bulky boot-like covering over the stirrups of a Western saddle confused me. Black Beauty responded nervously, sidling horse-knowingly.

"English saddle! Kapiolani Park!" Fred screeched like a scolding macaw. "Pull up your reins an' grab his mane! He's a big son-of-a-bitch! Grab! Grab! An' keep your hands off that pommel!" Fred screamed and rose to his feet. He was no longer taunting me. His tone was firm.

I made a final effort, rose easily above the saddle, and settled onto the highest horse I had ever mounted. Scrupulously careful in handling the reins, I took the horse around the yard in a smooth canter, reined him to a trot, and rode easily within Fred's view, careful to use every element of good horsemanship I had learned.

"We'll go for a short ride together in the back paddock," Fred said.

We rode until dusk.

"You're all right, boy! You ride pretty damned well! We'll go out next week after a pig. One of these days I'll bring home Fair Lady for you. Used to belong to Amy Baxter, the manager's daughter. A first-rate horse! Amy used to be a first-rate girl! Now she's married with two kids!"

We rode off before dawn. I felt like a kid out of school.

We stopped briefly in front of the pale green, white-trimmed house of Ikuwa Launui where Lepeka Lovelace lived. The house was silent and unlighted, surrounded by its wide unkempt lawns and tall trees, gray in the early morning mist.

"Hell, I'll stop this afternoon to see Lepeka! For all I know, she's still under the covers! I'm sure Ikuwa's already off up to Humuula after a pack of wild dogs that's raising hell." He studied the house for a moment and then gave it a grimace of reproof for not being lively the moment he appeared. Two pinto horses of beautiful markings grazed on the front lawn. A small flock of sheep clustered like a smoke-stained cloud. "We'll have to check some calves in Pookana II, an' then we'll see what pigs we can run down!"

"Those were beautiful pintos," I said.

"I don't like 'em. Get pintos and Hawaiians together an' they're like devils on a horse! Like Indians! They don't respect animals the way *we* do!"

Horses of the finest breeds abounded in Waimea, like the conifers and eucalyptus trees and the giants of native origin that blackened the mountain slopes: from the stream-lined, tapering-legged Thoroughbreds who grazed peacefully in the Puu-pueo paddocks, to the stylish bob-tailed saddle horse Judge Peyton rode and the compact husky herds of cowponies from which the remudas of the paniolos were made up. Like the thick spread of field and paddock, the abundant space, the cool air, the horses of Waimea added their grace, their elegance, and became an ingredient of the epic poetry of Waimea.

A gust of wind came on us suddenly as we loitered on the roadside.

"I've asked Kapua Gomes and Ernest Moluhi to ride with us. If anyone can ride down a boar, it's Moluhi! He's hell on horseback! A daredevil paniolo! Gomes is strong as a bull! Half-Portuguese. Mother is from a good old Waimea family." Fred spoke fast, high-pitched, and with bravura, bragging about male strength and daring.

We met the paniolos at a gate. Moluhi was stocky and quick; Gomes, as strong as his mount.

In the gullies, stunted lehua crowded against the remains of an ancient lava flow.

We came unexpectedly upon a small herd of wild pigs. Their leader, a rangy patriarchal boar of heroic size, had led the sows and their squealing shoats off some distance. Fred and Ernest Moluhi gave chase and cut out a yearling boar and a half-grown sow that Moluhi roped quickly.

"She looks damned good to me," said Fred.

Moluhi dismounted, hog-tied her, and attached her to the rear of his saddle. She weighed about seventy-five pounds.

Kapua Gomes galloped after the main herd, trying for a sow larger than Moluhi's. Fred lassoed a quite young boar, and called me to give him a hand.

I had been riding in all directions, trying to follow in the path first of one man and then another. In the chase I had unconsciously dug spurs into Black Beauty's glossy, ebony flanks. When I put my kaula-ili noose over the pig's neck, secured my end to the pommel and at Fred's orders dismounted, he caught sight of the slight rips made on his treasured animal's side. He began to say something, stopped, and then shrieked at the highest treble of his soprano: "Tie his legs, boy, tie his legs! I want to have a good look at this fella!" Fred stood over the pig, testing the sharpness of his dagger.

"Are you going to kill. . .?" I asked breathlessly.

"Hell no! I wanna put my mark on this fella! He's

too small to take home!" Fred bent over the squealing animal, swore at it, and deftly made a small triangular slit at the tip of one of its ears. "Untie the filthy little bastard, and look out! He's shitting all over the place!"

I avoided, as best I could, mingling my fingers with its fear-expelled excrement.

"Now loosen the nooses!" Fred ordered.

I stood near the animal as though to give it permission to leave. Once on its feet, it gave a swift glance around, settled on my boots, and charged my feet. Its tusks were mere butts, but its teeth were sharp, biting almost through to the skin of my ankles.

"Mount your horse, you stupid boy!" Fred screeched in fits of laughter.

"Ovah heah!" Moluhi was shouting.

Fred galloped off, and I followed, taking the opportunity to ride at full speed. Even on well-worn goat and pig trails, our legs rubbed against thorny stands of panini and barely escaped the sharp projections of the lava heaps.

Kapua Gomes was being chased on a grassy stretch outside the lava patch by the herd leader. He rode in zig-zag patterns, keeping just enough ahead of the boar to keep his horse's hind legs from being gored by the enormous stained tusks. Moluhi followed, cracking his whip to divert the huge pig's attention, but was handicapped by the sow slung behind his saddle.

With a burst of speed Fred took Duke into a small clearing to the side of Gomes and the boar, lassoed the pig, and secured the lariat to his saddle, while his horse planted its hooves. The boar spilled over nose first, hind feet high in the air, squealed, grunted, struggled to right itself, and was on its feet again before Gomes knew what had happened.

"Your rope, Moluhi!" Fred screeched.

Before the boar could make a charge, Moluhi's kaula-ili was pulled taut around its rangy neck. Kapua

Gomes reeled round and followed suit. The great beast tried desperately to cut itself free, but there was no way its tusks could reach the three tightly stretched lariats.

"Goddamned whore of a pig you were chasing was in heat! No wonder the boar came after you! Well, somebody's got to kill 'im now!" Fred ordered.

"Diz buggah eez mine!" Gomes said and leaped off his horse. His face was craggy like a pile of lava; his eyes, greenish and bloodshot.

"Watch your step, Kapua!" Fred warned—unnecessarily, I thought.

Gomes approached the boar directly and plunged his long dagger into its side. The pig screamed, sat on its haunches, and pawed the air. Gomes moved in for another thrust, but the pig reared.

"Rip his belly! " Fred screeched. "Let 'im kill himself!"

A gush of scarlet and pink spilled out of the great gash.

I turned away. I rode away. I began to feel myself losing consciousness. I wanted to cry.

"'Smatta, boy?" Fred called. "Ain't you ever seen one of these mean fuckers gutted before?"

I kept widening the distance.

In a short time Fred and the paniolos had run down the sow Gomes had been after and a yearling boar. They were secured tightly to the saddles, and we rode to a place near the highway.

Fred laughed for a long time, explaining in Hawaiian with gestures and guffaws, what had happened between me and the young boar before Moluhi had shouted for help. The paniolos joined in, but not so raucously or obviously. Later, Fred turned hard on me.

"Don't you ever, not ever, use spurs on that horse again, boy! Do you hear!"

"Yes, Uncle Fred," I mumbled.

"Where in the hell did you get those spurs, anyhow?"

"Julian gave them to me the night he left."

"Wouldn't you know it!" Fred said wearily. "Well, ride home and tell Joe to come after the pigs in the car. You come back with him to help. Get Georgie, too, if the little bugger's at home."

We left the pigs under a clump of lehua trees near a gate. "In two weeks time they'll be fat as butterballs," Fred said. "We'll have enough kalua pig to feed the whole Goddamned population of Waimea!"

Once out of sight I urged Black Beauty into a canter. Clouds of deep gray gathered over the region. I could see they were moving north in a warm kona. Before I reached the outskirts of the town, it had begun to thunder.

I had moved back to the bedroom given me originally. I now shared it with Henry who was asleep when Joe tiptoed in with Julian's letter, which had been addressed, as arranged, to him.

My greetings to you, haole boy from Honolulu:

If you forgive me please, I cannot remember what is you name. Real stupid head. Anyhow, my aloha to you. When you write to me I remembah you name an never moah address a lettah to you like diss.

How are tings in Waimea? Did you ride horse yet over that fine country aroun Waimea. I hope so because dat is why you told me so you came to Hawaii.

I am working on da ship Kamoi, da other one dat is taking pipi [cows] from Kawaihae to Honolulu. After da night I leave you I went Bens house makai of you uncle house on da way to Kawaihae. Da nex day I come Kawaihae wheah I meet da preacher Mr. Kaauwai. I tell him all my troubles. When da Kamoi come to port da captain tell Mr. Kaauwai he need coupla mans. I talk to da captain, one Hawaiian from Kauai, an he give me da job. I am a pretty good sailor for somebody who nevah sail da seven seas before. Any how I like my job I glad be gone Waimea. Only ting how is Puna? I theenk of him, I dream of him. Diss boy is my special love. I miss him very much. I worry like hell bout his sick, but when we come back from Honolulu aftah my firs trip da cowboys from home say Puna is now alright. Thanks be to God. I think I be coming up Waimea for da horse race on fourth of July. May be I see you an Puna when I come.

I know you help take care Puna. You one very kine boy an my aloha will always be in my heart foah you. Take care Puna an give my love to da other two churrens.

When you write lettah to me sent to:—

Reverend Noah Kaauwai
Box 11
Kawaihae, Hawaii

Piha, piha loa o ka puuwai iau. You understan? Ask Joe if you no can figgah out what that mean.

My aloha to you from all my heart
Julian K. Lono

"Maybe now his heart is at peace," said Joe.

"Pololei paha, aale polole paha," I said, falling into the habit now of using short Hawaiian phrases when I talked to Joe.

"Pololei, it's true! Mahalo a nui loa, O Jesu Cristo. Thanks be to da Lord. He knows all our trouble. If you write Julian one lettah, you geev um to me an' I sen' to heem."

He did not disturb the dogs as he left.

Sleepily I composed my answer, sitting at the edge of the four-poster, bundled and belted tightly into my dressing gown. First, I told him my name. Then I went into a lengthy description of the horses that had been chosen for me to ride. Fred had repeated that Julian was afraid of unbroken horses, meaning he did not conform to the Waimea ideal of malehood.

But during our ride for oranges, something in the way Julian managed reins, and sat, made me feel he was at ease on horseback. I wrote how well Puna had recovered, knowing Julian's intense, loving interest in the boy. I did not mention the fire ball, nor the peculiar behavior of Laura and Louise.

I wrote that Fred had asked Lepeka Lovelace and her sister to help prepare a luau.

Julian's answer arrived two days later.

Dear Markie: (you don' mine if I call you like dis?)

I get your letter from Reverend Kaauwai befoah we leave there da other day. You make me shame da way you write so good. Me I write like one damn fool Kawaihae. But my heart feel good somebody I know can write like you so long as you no mine the way I write.

I am so glad to here bout Puna. I ask God every day for help him. If I could I come see him right now. My job keep me bizzy when we at Kawaihae. Only half day any how. But my heart is happy for Puna. You tell him I come Waimea one of these days soon. I bring him some ting from Honolulu. May be God angry witt Fred an me an he punish us with Punas sick. You take care him. Give him plenny poi, plenny milk.

Honolulu is good place someways and bad place other ways. My pals from da ship they go bline when we hit Honolulu. Plenny bars on Kekaulike and Maunakea Street. Twice I go wit them I drink so much I forget how I get to the place I sleep. I have one room on King Street neah da car barn. Small room but nough for me. I can not sleep because too much noise an da smell from so many cars I cannot get use to.

I'm coming Waimea for sure on July 4. I don know what time I be there—but I be there. You tell Puna I see him soon. Thass if F. not aroun' when I comin thru.

My aloha to you, Markie, until I see you again wit my own eyes.

Your friend,
Julian K. Lono

I told Puna only that Joe had received a letter from Julian who was working on a ship.

"Uncle Julian on one boat?" he cried out happily. Fantasies would keep him joyously occupied for days.

Fred's ravings against Julian never stopped. Late in the evening or while we rode alone together, he addressed his remarks to me, and would try to be analytical.

"Julian has all the traits of a good-for-nothing Hawaiian. There are plenty of them. Read the newspapers! More than half the people who get in dutch with the law are Hawaiians. Julian's so stealthy. Take the time he was in your bedroom, lighting the lamp. So cheeky, really! Arrogant! He had no business going in there. These kanakas have lots of cunning, sit around all day looking so sly, and so above it all when you see them in Kona or Hilo."

"What about the cowboys?" I asked boldly.

"They're old school! You couldn't find a cleaner-minded bunch!" He paused. "Not the younger crop mind you! The fellas coming on the ranch now are the young Japs and Portugees and mixed breeds of every color."

There was a long pause. I tried to assemble the scattered fragments of my Uncle's rantings. I failed.

"I tried my darndest to get that fella to learn cowpunching. He's gotta yellow streak. Scared as hell of horses. Afraid of busting his ass on a bucking horse, I guess."

What compelled me most was that Fred recited as though his excoriations were prayers. He had found his Prince of Darkness in Julian.

Lepeka's first appearance at Fred's house was like the wild peacock I had seen flying from one wili-wili to another at Manulani. She came in a much-ruffled and fitted white madras holoku: a long dress with wrist to shoulder fitted sleeves and high neck line, in which rural Hawaiian women were so beguiling. Lepeka's golden ehu hair was piled high and caught at the back by a nosegay of white and yellow ginger that at once made fragrant the entire house. Her green eyes were more playful in their liveliness than suspecting or furtive, the impression one usually has from restless eyes: *makahi'a* eyes, as the Hawaiians express it, compared to *maka 'eu*. In fact *maka lea*, wandering or eager eyes, might be more accurate for Lepeka's. When they settled on you, they made your skin tingle; they made you erotic. Her silk-smooth skin was as golden as her hair. Her cheeks wore a constant blush. Her voice, though throaty, was marvelously toned. Her frequent laughter came from a sustained sense of pleasure.

"All my life I live in this country, and this is the second time I been in this house," were her first words, which, with a toss of the head, a movement of an arm, a look, gently rebuked Fred and his isolated way of life. Floods of utterances in beautiful sounding Hawaiian phrases gave her reactions as Fred conducted her on a quick tour of the downstairs rooms. When they reached the breakfast-dining room, she said:

"Dish! Plenny dish is what you need for luau!"

"We got plenty of them," Fred said. "The china closet's full!"

"How about paper plates, Uncle Fred?" I volunteered, dreading the possible destruction of Aunt Louise's still intact sets.

"Nana oe i keia keiki—malama nui o ka dishes of da aunty!"

"Paper plates cost too damned much! Why put out money for something when you don't need!"

Fred served Lepeka a drink, and soon after, another. We talked monotonously about the china, I suspected, because I was there. I excused myself and left them with the Bohemian glass decanter half full of oke.

I found Joe at the pig pen finishing the noisy feeding. The wild pigs we had brought back mingled among their domesticated brethren and grew fat for the luau.

"You uncle, I teenk he like one noo wife!"

"Perhaps."

"Goodlooking buggah, na wahine maka lalau o ka lau woho ehu!"

"Don't you want a wife and children, Joe?"

"Au'we," he answered. "I'm one *maka ka ka'a*, one cock-eye! Churren? Look aroun' you!" he motioned with his arm. "Da pua'a, da ilio, da hawsses. You folks ma. Dass all my churren!" He laughed and muttered, as he stacked the slop cans.

"You come from Waipio, too, eh, Joe?"

"I come from Waimanu, mauka of Waipio. Small

keed time, my paren's move down Waipio. We live dere few yeah, an' we move away. Me move aftah my faddah die."

"How did he die?"

"Au'we, Markie, you one real niele!" he laughed. "my faddah die from hoohewahewa. Hoomana kolohe. You know what iss dat?"

"Kahuna."

"A oia no! Plenny peoples die from dat."

"My uncle . . ." I started.

"Aale walaau. Me, I doan know nutting. He treat me good. In some way, he iss a werry good man," he said and fell silent. He scanned the dark skies. "Wheah dose damn keeds?" He called out to them, showing the routine Hawaiian dread at the coming of night.

At that point we heard Fred and Lepeka's risque laughing from the kitchen porch.

"Joe! Joe! Hele mai! Come here! Where are you?" Fred called.

Joe called back and then said to me "He like me take da wahine ehu home. You come wit me, Markie?"

"I'll wait till you come back before we have dinner," I said, hoping that would appease him.

After a jolly dinner, Fred came to my bedroom with the remains of the decanter and two jigger glasses and settled into his favorite rocking chair. He poured one jigger full and the other about half.

"We'll have a drink to Lepeka! One of the prettiest women I've ever seen!"

He drank.

"Just sip it, boy. Booze is wonderful stuff, if it doesn't ruin your life. I've been a heavy drinker all my life, but I've never missed a day of work or been too sick to get out of bed. Hawaiians can't handle liquor." The judgment seemed to please him.

"I'm glad Lepeka—I mean, Miss Lovelace— is going to help with the luau."

"Now why are you glad of that?" he asked, scratched his scrotum, and poured himself another drink.

"She seems to know what she's doing, and she's very pleasant."

"A country-type Hawaiian woman—hard working, frugal, and full of common sense!"

"She really is a beautiful woman," I said. "A true half-white beauty!"

"Now what do *you* know about 'true half-white beauties,' eh, boy? You felt around the girls yet?"

I kept my silence.

"C'mon, boy. Hell, when your father and I were your age, we were already lovin' them up! That's what life's about for a man!" He cackled, poured himself another drink, and looked at me studiedly. "You get a hard on when you see a pretty woman?"

My cheeks flushed.

"Now, c'mon, boy. You're old enough to be asked that!"

"Sometimes," I squeaked.

"Sometimes! That's good!" He howled. "We were devils! One thing I can't understand," he continued, "is people playing with themselves! You can go crazy doing it! Do you do it, boy?"

"No."

"And another thing I can't for the life of me tolerate are these Goddamned mahus . . . fall in love with their own sex!" Fred's voice squeaked and cracked. He reached again for the decanter, which was nearly empty. "I've long suspected that son-of-a-bitch who recently left this house. That's why I told you to leave him alone!" He leaned forward in the rocking chair, leering. "That's why I didn't like the idea of him being in your room!"

I was speechless.

"Don't look at me with that look of sweet innocence, Mark Hull! I know you think I'm not being right to Lepeka. You looked at me as if I didn't respect her this afternoon. Don't jump to conclusions! Part of respecting her is wanting to seduce her, because she is a beautiful woman who's gone too long without a man! Now you mark my words, Markie, a man has got to seduce women to be a man! They hate your guts if you don't!"

Fred was drunk. His face was florid. I summoned courage and rose from my chair.

"Don't hate me, boy, for saying these things! Life is full of dangers. Sooner or later, we have to learn the facts of life," he mumbled as I led him from my room.

I was shaking with rage. We reached his bed, and he sploshed onto it like an over-ripe pomelo falling from the higher branches of the tree outside into the silky turf of St. Augustine grass below.

I rode out with Fred twice during the following week, high on the northern slopes of Mauna Kea. We talked most of the time about his impending luau.

"I can borrow a big closed tent from the ranch. Their luau is on the Fourth, a week before mine," Fred said, and swept his gaze across the fields.

"Anyway, they use the Ellen Kiliwehi Stevenson Hall."

The ranch's annual Fourth of July celebration had been initiated by Albert Baxter who, as a very young man, had participated in the revolutionary events that toppled the Hawaiian throne and led eventually to annexation. In our family annals, he was no friend.

"You'll need ferns for the tables . . . and flowers."

"Lepeka and the womenfolk will take care of all that! Gomes and Moluhi and a coupla others are going up the Mahike forest. We'll have maile leis for everyone! I'm going to ask Anita Warrington and her grandsons to come. Also the Baxters. You know who Mrs. Warrington is?"

"Yes, she's the grandmother of the Dinwiddie twins who inherited the Stevenson Ranch when their mother died."

"By golly, you do know! She's the reigning queen of this whole ranch! Her grandsons are under her guardianship. Their mother was Anita Warrington's only child. Kiliwehi Stevenson! Her father was Lemuel Stevenson, the third."

"He was a younger brother of Tony Stevenson who died young," I said.

"How did you know that?" he demanded.

"He was engaged to my Great-aunt Sybil Hull who became Mrs. Henry Newton. They were engaged to be married when he met with the fatal accident."

Fred gestured with an arm. "Right above us in that rugged open country, too high for trees. He was going after one of the stallions my father had sold them. I remember him quite well. His brothers, Lemuel and Daniel, inherited the ranch after he died. Dan sold out to Lemuel for eight hundred thousand. Lemuel married Anita and brought her here to live. She was from a Honolulu family."

"She was a Dawson," I said.

"That's right! How did you know?"

"The Dawson girls were close friends of my Aunt Elsie Kennedy. Also her aunts, Eudora and Sybil. They all went to school in California. The Blessed Virgin Seminary, or something."

"You know quite a lot about the old folks, boy! You'll be living in the past the rest of your life, if you don't watch out!"

Fred made no notes on his ranch inspections, but each trouble and its location were kept in his memory like a detailed photograph for whoever would be sent to make repairs.

As we made our descent, a fog blew across the grassy slopes, unevenly in successive sheets of moist air. Through this moody coolness, I spotted two groupings of trees surrounding more-or-less square areas; one, considerably larger than the other. The dark green squares would be visible for a few moments and then be shrouded by fog.

"One is the burial place of the Stevenson family—the other surrounds the old homestead, Puu-malu," Fred said.

We stopped at the graveyard site, removed our hats, but stayed mounted, engulfed sporadically by the swirls of fog.

"They're all here—the Stevensons! Babies, children, old Ebenezer, the First, Lemuel, Kiliwehi—all of 'em!"

"Uncle Tony Stevenson, too?"

"Yes, but maybe you shouldn't call him that while you're up here. People might get the idea that you were claiming to be related."

"I have enough relatives," I said. "Uncle Tony" was a hero to those of us of the younger generation who had been exposed to Great-aunt Sybil's poignant reveries.

"We'll take a look at Puu-malu," Fred said shortly.

Within the larger, two-hundred-yard square bordered by enormous evergreen trees were several small buildings and, rising out of the luxuriant growth, the stone foundations of an huge house.

"They had two bad fires here."

I was reminded of Southern mansions gutted in the War Between the States. I had seen photographs of Puu-malu in its days of glory: gay parties assembled on a broad verandah, in the gardens, or on horseback on the drive; beautiful people expensively dressed. In yellowing photographs of our own ranch at Manulani, people wore the same look of ease, privilege, and, caught in leisured enjoyment of good fortune, hidden under languid smiles, a suggestion that their world would soon disappear.

"My grand-uncles and aunts came here in the old days."

"Everybody that was anybody in the islands used to come to Puu-malu!" Fred said testily.

"World-famous people, too!" I said. "Jack London, the Prince of Wales, Alice Roosevelt!"

"Oh, yes, those."

Cutting across a field, our horses half-lost in the deep grasses, we saw a group of horsemen going toward Puu-malu, led by two young men on matched chestnut-colored horses ahead of an enormous limousine.

"The heirs!" Fred swept his free arm through the air.

"The Dinwiddie twins."

"Poor kids! They come here for a few weeks in the summer, generally, once a year. Once or twice they were kept away for two or three years at a stretch! Look at that big car!"

It was a town car with an open driver's seat, separated by a sheath of glass from the sedan.

"She follows them wherever they go—their grandmother, Anita Warrington. They've been brought up like hothouse plants!"

"She lost her husband and daughter, their mother," I said.

"Yes, also lost Warrington, her second husband. An Englishman I think he was. But Kiliwehi's children. . . She shouldn't treat 'em like delicate ferns! Eben's a born horseman! He could make a real rancher someday."

"Their father, Dinwiddie, was from a prominent Southern family."

"He was a damned beast! A brute to Kiliwehi. Don't know why she ever married 'im! The marriage was considered one of the great all-time disasters in

Hawaii. Their grandmother insists they pay respects to their poor dead mother's memory at least once when they come here."

"I've heard she died in London."

'Well you heard wrongly. It was in Paris, France. What do you know about the Baxters?"

"They both come from Honolulu. Albert Baxter's mother came from a missionary family. Mrs. Baxter's people, the Hartleys, were in the sugar business."

"I bet you don't know this!" he said, looking sly. "Your father's people, the Hulls, negotiated with Albert Baxter to run *their* ranches after Edward Hull's death in San Francisco!"

"He injured his leg and went there for treatment. He died at the Palace Hotel before they could get hime into the hospital."

"Well, his brothers were arguing among themselves and agreeing on nothing when old Sam Dawson, Anita's father, plucked him from the Hulls and brought hime here after Lemuel's death. Lem died in New York of pneumonia. He and Anita were returning from a trip to Europe. His mother, Hannah Stevenson, wailed and grieved for years. Anita returned with their only child. Kiliwehi grew up, married Dinwiddie, and travelled a lot. She died in Paris. Pneumonia again—same thing that killed her father. The twin boys were left in her mother's care."

"Why did Mr. Dawson want to take Mr. Baxter away from the Hulls?" I was now much more interested in my own family.

"Baxter was the best Goddamned rancher here. He was given a free hand, nobody to interfere. There were too many of you Goddamned Hulls running things! Look at what he's made of this ranch! You people would have been as rich as these boys if Baxter had managed the Hull lands."

Manulani and Makuakai had been converted by

others into fields of sugar cane and pineapple.

"Is it true Lemuel Stevenson was prayed to death?" I asked.

"Nothing but bullshit! I want to tell you something, boy, for your own good! These matters should not be talked about. They belong to the old days, and only to the people concerned! Hawaiians are deeply respectful people Unless a person is sure of something, they don't like to hear him talk about it. They call it waha kani, or waha he'e! Remember this, boy." Fred looked at me sternly, "And don't you ever forget it."

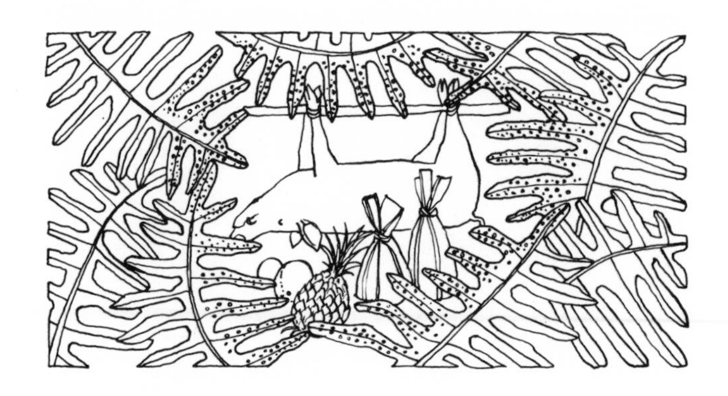

Lepeka came ostensibly to plan and prepare for Puna's birthday luau, but everyone enjoyed the idea that these meetings were acts of courtship, that Fred was in hot pursuit of his fourth wife. "Let 'em talk! Let 'em talk!" Lepeka would say between outbursts of nervous laughter. It was obvious that after her long captivity of caring for ailing parents, she was ready to assume the risks of becoming Fred's fourth wife.

Sometimes Lepeka came with her sister Piilani Launui. Their laughter filled the old rooms; their beauty brought back the old grace and charm. Piilani spoke better English, so talked more freely about Waimea and the history of her own and other local families. The original Lovelace, an Englishman, had settled early in the Kohala area. He married a sister of the first Mrs. Stevenson: a genealogical item of great importance.

"We are of the same family," Piilani said one day, "but our side has never been rich."

"Our family's the same way," I said. "Some rich, some poor, some in the middle."

"Oh my, the Hulls have always been rich! I can remember my grandfather speaking of old man Hull and old man Arlington and their shipyard at the bottom of Fort Street."

"That was divided up and sold many years ago."

"But there was *plenny* of land in the Hull family. Like your cousin Fred here!" She gestured towards him. "My goodness, he has land all over this island!"

Lepeka smiled and said: "He kind man, you cousin!"

"He could be kinder, if he wanted to be," Piilani scolded.

One day Hanford and his wife Gerta brought a supply of pots and pans, giving Hanford an opportunity to come and see for himself what was happening between his father and Lepeka Lovelace. Hanford towered well above six feet, his bulk, massive, typically Hawaiian. He and his brother Ben had attended a mid-Western university and played football.

"So you're the towhead from Honolulu," was his greeting. "My wife and Dad say you've been doing the cooking around here."

"Everyone liked your chili pie recipe," I said to Gerta.

"You here alone? Where are the kids?" Hanford asked.

"Upstairs with Mrs. Launui and her sister."

"He must be off his rocker, giving this luau! You say they're upstairs?"

We walked into the breakfast room, Hanford's eyes, small, restless and distrusting, sweeping in all directions. He was maka ni-o.

Hanford went to the landing and called. "Hui! Hui! Anybody up there?"

The children came to the head of the stairs and said nothing.

"What you doing up there?" Hanford said.

Piilani Launui came into view, dishevelled from

her labors. "Oh it's you, Hanford! My sister Becky and I are here helping clean up the place."

"Old place needs it."

Piilani quickly resumed command of herself. "Hello, Gerta!" she called down pleasantly. "You folks coming up?"

"No, no," Hanford answered. "I have to see someone in Kona about designing a new bridge." He was an engineer with the government.

When we had finished lunch, Piilani said to me, "This is a peculiar family. I know they're your cousins, but have you known them long? I have a feeling nothing has been touched in those rooms upstairs since Miriam died. Even before that perhaps. She was a very frail woman."

"It would take a staff of servants to keep this house in good condition," I said.

"Lissen to Sonny, how smaht he talk!" Lepeka contributed.

"You are smart, Markie. And you must excuse the way my sister talks. She was the only one who didn't go to Honolulu for schooling. Four of us graduated from Kamehameha. Two of my sisters and I went on to the Normal School for teachers training. Where do you go to school? Punahou?"

"All those snotty haoles that go there!" said Lepeka.

Puna and Leihulu charged into the room. "Auntie Laura and Auntie Louise coming!"

"Au'we, I must go comb my hair."

The sisters dashed into Fred's "mother's bathroom."

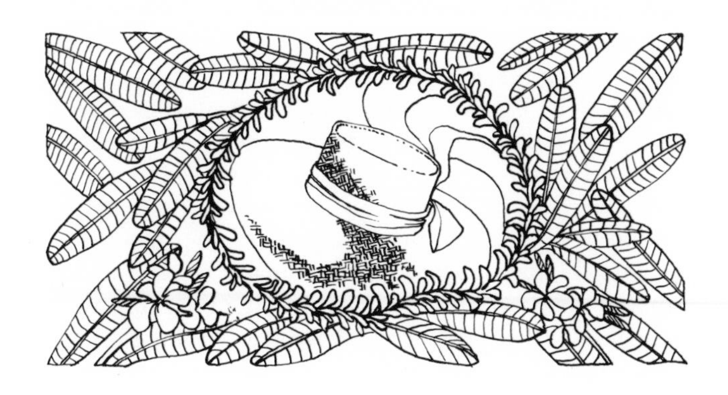

As the Fourth of July fell on Wednesday, the events sponsored by the ranch were held off until the weekend. Horse races were run on Saturday and Sunday with a dance culminating the first day's events and a "Grand Luau," those of the second.

Fred escorted Lepeka gallantly. She wore her gold and black pa'u for the Grand Parade preceding the first day's racing events, and rode one of her brother-in-law Ikuwa Launui's pintos. Piilani rode the other, in a matching costume. They were both crowned with pua makahala leis made from flowers gathered at Fred's. Their necks and shoulders and those of their mounts were decked with long-leafed maile from Panaewa forest near Hilo. Two other sisters, who had come up from Honolulu by the little cattle boat, wore scarlet velvet pa'us trimmed in black; on their heads were leis of red lehua; symbolic flower of the volcanic Big Island, the favorite blossom of Pele, goddess of fire. The four sisters were cheered when they rode past the grandstand and again when they took their places next to us.

The Dinwiddie twins rode in on their matched chestnut-colored horses amidst a company of young cowboy grooms. The boys wore white riding outfits and flowing black capes and Stetson hats banded with lauhala leis. They also wore hala leis entwined with many strands of maile around their necks. Gold tasselled red sashes around their waists gave a final flourish of festivity to their appearance. I thought I would never see anything so dramatic, so princely and elegant as the appearance they made. Their tanned smooth skins were pulled taut; their eyes, very dark and luminous. They bore a likeness to one another but were not identical twins. Eben sat his horse with authority, his hands strong and quiet. Uncle Tony Stevenson! I thought. I knew then why Fred, the cowboys, and other people always talked of him as the one to take over the ranch when he came of age.

I turned to the nearby box with striped red, white, and blue bunting draped across it, and recognized their grandmother sitting and smiling in queenly self-possession. How I ached with jealousy. My great-aunt Sybil might have been the reigning queen of the day at Waimea had "Uncle Tony" lived; and my cousins Stanton, Dick, and Charlie Newton, her grandsons all, be riding in the place of the twins. And me!

Just before the day's last race was run, I was presented to Mrs. Warrington and her grandsons. She wore her usual costume, a white silk dress and large veiled leghorn hat. Her hands were gloved.

"We've met at my Aunt Elsie's on Beretania Street," I reminded her.

"Elsie Hull Kennedy! Of course! How is dear Elsie? I haven't seen her since we've been back. So you're young Mark's son! Of course. There was old old Mark, old Mark, and then young Mark! You should be young young Mark!"

It sounded Chinese and was amusing. I liked her regal airs, the rich tone of her British speech, her hauteur which reflected her descent from the ranking chiefs of old. She helped me regain the self-possession I had begun to lose with my Waimea cousins who had lost the style of the old court families. Under more usual circumstances these dowagers could make one want to race out of large, high-ceilinged, dark rooms to the freedom of the sea or playing field.

"I want you to meet my grandsons."

They were sitting nearby in conversation with beautifully dressed guests. "This is Mark Hull, fourth, darlings. He's from the Hull family. I went to school with his grand-aunts and his aunt, Elsie Hull Kennedy. This is Eben," she said.

His grip was like a vise; his smile, great. "Hello, Mark. It's good to meet you. This is my brother Lemuel Gaylord Dinwiddie," he said teasingly. "He likes to be called Gaylord!"

Gaylord greeted me with a cool, almost imperceptible nod.

"Perhaps we could ride together someday?" Eben asked.

"Grandmother says we're leaving next week," Gaylord said peevishly. "She has business in Honolulu."

"The new stallion won't be arriving until the end of next week, or later."

"I hope we don't have to stay here that long. There's not even a movie house here. I haven't seen a film in over three weeks."

"Did you say a new stallion?" I said.

"Golden Fleece, a colt of Gold Oak of the Gullion Farms in Kentucky. We bought him on the way home this trip. Mr. Baxter met us in Kentucky. Hasn't been a stud here worth his keep since Grandpa died."

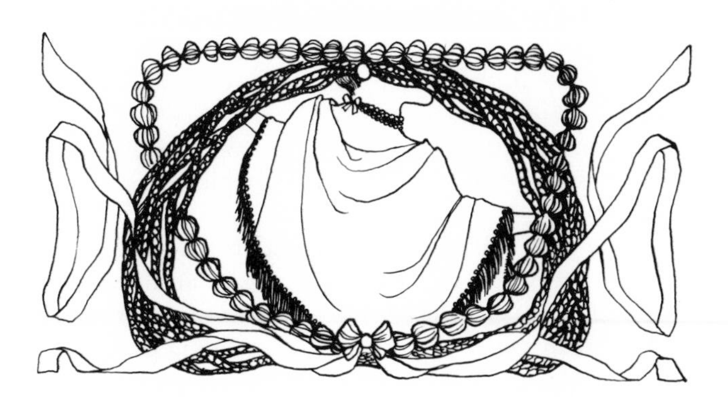

We dined on a huge leg of mutton I had roasted in the morning. Fred ferreted out of the pantry a bottle of mango chutney that dated back to his mother's times. "Don't know why I keep so much old stuff around here, but, by God, it comes in handy at a time like this. Try some, boy! It'll not only put hair on your chest, it'll be the best tastin' chutney you were ever lucky enough to eat!" I recognized the recipe Judge Aylett had brought from England in 1850. We had Portuguese sweet bread (purchased from a booth at the races) and poha jam and guava jelly for dessert.

"Quite a gal, that Nita Warrington. She never changes!" Fred laughed. "That hat! Big enough to cap Mauna Loa! And gloves!" he sputtered, catching his breath between squeals. "And that old fox Baxter was playin' up to her like nobody's business all day! Wonder what he's after now? And that old pua'a laho Ikuwa! Flirtin' like hell with his wife's sisters!" He imitated Ikuwa Launui's slightly lisping speech, his extravagantly old-fashioned manners.

The children sat in their usual midnight silence, but their eyes glowed.

"Quite a sight, eh, boy? our Waimea horse races?

What horses! What riders!" He flailed his arms. "Speed and form! What more do you want from a Thoroughbred?"

"You want them to win," I said thoughtlessly. The most beautiful animals in a couple of heats had come in last.

Joe had talked for days about the clothes he intended to wear and the fragrant pak lan flowers he had chosen for his hat lei. He had used the buds which would keep their form during the evening even if he would remove his hat moments after he reached Ellen Kiliwehi Stevenson Hall.

"These public events are very important to the people here," Fred said. "There's nothing else to do. Hawaiians are real dudes—the old-fashioned ones, I mean, not the moe-lepos, your louts."

Joe would ride his horse to the dance along with many of the younger ranch hands: a kind of status in his circle. Fred, in the Packard, which Joe had brought to a high gloss, picked up Lepeka and her sisters. Ikuwa would follow later on one of the pintos. The women were stunning in trailing holokus of flower-patterned silk jersey cloth, pikake headband leis, necklaces and earrings of kukui nut, palaoa of whale bone, and Niihau shells. Piilani and Mercedes, the elder sister from Honolulu, wore tortoise shell combs that fanned handsomely above their pikake crowns.

"Now I've got the four queens of Kohala, I think we ought to drive to Kilauea and spend the weekend at the Volcano House!" Fred shouted.

"Listen to Fred! Kolohe oe!" Mercedes Kaia teased.

"I've never been to the Volcano House! Let's go!" Mary Ann Alonzo, the other Honolulu sister, meant what she said. She had a slight tough masculinity.

Fred's defenses had been weakened by the engulfing presence of "the queens of Kohala." "If I wasn't planning to give a luau next week, I'd drive to Hilo without batting an eye! The boy here hasn't been to Hilo or the volcano!"

One of the sisters broke into Hawaiian, and, for the rest of the drive, a whole saga was narrated between explosions of laughter. I caught bits of phrasing, a word here and there, but for the most part the exchanges might just as well have been in Croatian or Greek. They spoke in the old-fashioned, annoying, elusive metaphors, which I ached to understand more completely, although they touched on matters erotic that did not yet deeply interest me: big round balls of breadfruit suitably wrinkled, the plunging prow of a canoe, the delicate flesh of mangoes, the pink of some flowers, the rushing of winds, a ship coming full sail into port.

Fred nearly choked in squeaks of delight. Before we reached the hall, he had convinced the Honolulu sisters to stay and help Lepeka prepare his luau.

"Give us enough money and a free hand, Palani, and we'll show them how folks from Kohala do things!" Mary Ann challenged Fred, whose penuriousness was legendary. After a barely audible grunt, he capitulated gracefully.

All of Waimea and a host of people from Honokaa and Kona came to the dance as dates, guests, or relatives of people employed at the Stevenson Ranch. The "queens of Kohala" were soon surrounded by admirers of both sexes and all ages. Fred beamed euphorically, a tower of pride in white cashmere breeches and English boots, charged with the spirit of the finest stallion on the Pookanaka range, surrounded by his willing brood of elegant mares. For his Stetson, Lepeka had woven a lei of roses with palapalai fern, the pointed tips of which spilled over the brim and trembled gently as he moved.

I melted into the periphery of the scented, handsome, chattering circle, which soon sailed into the hall like old-time chiefs on occasions of state. I had wanted them to stay posed forever.

Ellen Kiliwehi Stevenson Hall, one of the few buildings in Waimea with electricity, was used for many purposes but most actively as a gymnasium. Basketball nets hung from the rafters. A small stage was equipped for simple theatrical productions. The brown velvet curtains were a recent gift from Mr. and Mrs. Baxter. Tonight, in special honor of Mrs. Warrington and her grandsons, who had not been here for the two previous Fourth of July celebrations, evergreen branches adorned the verandah posts, braided fern hung from the basketball goals, and strings of maile festooned the stage curtain. At either side of the proscenium stood, stiffly but resplendently, kahili standards made from masses of orange day lilies and green ti leaves, stuck into chicken wire. In the old days, kahilis made from feathers had an individual character and bore sacred, mystical names. Our ancestors would have been appalled at their being used as decoration, devoid of their traditional significance. The sight of the chicken wire kahili that night and their display in the event and the place gave me a jolt.

Bobby Ahlo's Serenaders—guitar, drums, bass, two saxophones, and a trumpet (Bobby Ahlo's instrument)—had been imported from Hilo. They were a raffish crew in pale-blue dinner jackets, white trousers, and maile leis flung round their shoulders. They played the hits of the day, and the frequency of the flat notes, the inadvertent disharmonies, established their "sound," so typical of island dance bands of the thirties, carrying me back to high school proms, those dances held at plantation gymnasiums or to the old Armory on Hotel Street where we went on rare occasions to catch a glimpse of the masses at play.

The dance was in full swing, but an air of decorum fell over the little hall with the arrival of Mrs. Warrington and her party. A tune stopped prematurely as Bobby Ahlo's schooled eye caught sight of the gentry at the entrance. Dancers swiftly and quietly left the floor. Bursts of laughter ceased; talk was restrained. The combination of Sunday School manners and old-fashioned respect was in keeping with the character of Waimea and its people who lived generally in some economic relation to the ranch. The dance became a chic, private party.

In dignified procession, Mrs. Warrington, her twin grandsons, and their guests, crossed the floor and took their places in wicker chairs set in the bower-alcove arranged for them near the stage. The tall, heavyish dowager, joined now by several women her own age (some of whom I could identify), wore a black lace holoku of elaborate cut with a long train. She had wrapped around her shoulders a black silk Chinese shawl, heavily weighted with embroidery. A leihulu of exquisite yellow feathers sat like a crown atop her gray hair, and around her neck sparkled a choker of diamonds and emeralds. Diamond earrings of marquise-cut dangled from her pierced ears. On one wrist she wore a huge boar's tusk bracelet edged with gold upon which, in letters of jet, her Hawaiian name was emblazoned. The other hapa-haole women of her party were similarly dressed, but with no such splendor. The twins wore conventional suits: Lemuel Gaylord in white linen, Eben in pale-blue palm beach. I was relieved, as I suppose Eben was, that they were not a matched pair. The Baxters, their son, their unmarried daughter, and several older haole couples, were in conventional evening clothes.

A group of paniolos and their women came in with guitars and ukeleles and formed a half-circle in front of the twins and their grandmother. For a moment an air of uncertainty swept through the ranks of the music makers. Were there too many strangers among Anita Warrington's guests? With superior aplomb, a tall, dark-haired woman began to strum her ukulele and let her beautiful voice form the words and music of a song written by one of the very early Stevenson women.

Mrs. Warrington looked pleased, although the infusion of melancholy was unmistakable. What memories had the song brought back to her? Always these shreds of the past enter our lives in Hawaii to sting, to prick, to hurt. I looked sternly at the flower kahili flanking the bedecked alcove. I thought Mrs. Warrington caught my glance. I turned away.

Fred seemed under a spell, thrust briefly out of his world of hardtack, dawn risings to check pasturelands, and long horseback rides, high above the swaying mist-gray lehua, in lonely contemplation of the beauties and wonders of Waimea. Lepeka and her sisters drifted in the same motionless veneration. Hawaiian songs too often were a harkening to the past, to your people, reminding you always of breakdown and defeat.

I studied Lemuel Gaylord, whose glacial indifference comforted me. Perhaps we all needed to be a little more indifferent; we whose lives were rooted in the indigenous compost heap of island history.

The group completed several songs in honor of members of the Stevenson family, their homes, their past deeds. One or two songs were mercifully spirited, even gay. Mrs. Warrington, in an attractive attitude that suggested composure and enjoyment, nodded her approval. Others in her party clapped with studied restraint.

There was a nervous conferring among the serenaders, and Lepeka and her sisters came forth. Mrs. Warrington beckoned to Fred to join her and he left my side. When he reached her, she motioned with a lovely sweep of her arm (the one with the boar's tooth bracelet) for me to come as well. The Lovelace sisters, famous for their singing of the songs of Kohala, began a composition of Piilani's in honor of the pua makahala flower. Their voices were in close harmony; their pronunciation, perfect: "I have plucked you dew drenched in the early morning and fashioned you into wreaths, small and large; wreaths that adorned my head in childhood; wreaths now for the treasured shoulders of my loved one. Pua makahala, dainty but strong! Pua makahala telling of my love so that I am spared the need to speak of it." There was rousing applause. Even Mrs. Warrington clapped. It was a rare treat for the people of Waimea to hear the Lovelace sisters singing as a foursome again. Even more, perhaps, their collective beauty was a joy to see.

"They sing *mai nei loko,* from the heart!" Mrs. Warrington said in a choked voice.

"They do, indeed," Fred responded, his voice squeaking like a rusty lock.

"I remember, Palani, when you and your friends used to sing for your mother, dear Louise." Now her voice had its usual firmness.

"Oh my, that was years ago," Fred chuckled.

"I'll never forget your singing. It was beautiful. I was a young bride and spent many pleasant days with Aunt Louise and the girls."

She turned a familiar queenly gaze on me. So many women of her generation of the old court families had this particular look: a mixture of femme fatale and grand duchess; of hauteur behind which lurked an element of Polynesian eroticism. "Do you remember your cousin's mother, Aunt Louise?" Mrs. Warrington asked me in a friendly way. "No, of course you wouldn't. She died years ago. A most fascinating woman. Very bright. She doctored people all over this section of the island. She'd been trained, I think, by the very first English sisters to come here. Am I correct, Fred?"

"Yes, yes, that's true. Back in the eighteen-sixties, I think."

I lifted my eyes from feasting on Mrs. Warrington's feather lei and jewels, and looked, for no particular reason, across the heads of the people surrounding us, toward the front entrance. I saw Julian Lono slip into the hall.

"You will excuse me, Aunt Nita, if you please?" Fred said nervously.

My blood chilled.

"Eben tells me he wants to ride with you, Mark. I don't encourage the boys to ride off alone. Of course, if you both promise to be careful and agree to ride with a groom, I'll give my consent."

My eyes anxiously tried to search through labyrinths of towering hairdos, leis, red neckerchiefs, to locate Julian.

"Au'we, now that the serenading is over, we must be going, paha?" Mrs. Warrington said in the old-fashioned way. "But how do you like Waimea, Mark?" I heard her question but failed to respond immediately. "Do you like Waimea?" she repeated.

"I love it," I blurted. "Waimea is the most fascinating place I've ever seen."

"It's a lonely place, a forlorn place, a very strange, even haunting place in some ways," the patrician matriarch said as though reciting an elegy. Then her voice became harsh. "It's hardly a place for civilized young men to grow up. There are too many dangers." She looked me straight in the eye. You understand, young, young Mark, she seemed to be saying. I think I do, I responded, without speaking.

Eben came over. "Real Waimea singing—the best!"

Lemuel Gaylord now lurked behind his grandmother, acknowledging my presence with a jerk of his head. "Time to be going, don't you think, Grandmamma?"

As Mrs. Warrington made the first cumbersome movements of leave-taking, common to such occasions, I said goodnight and went in search of Julian. He was not in the hall. I found Fred hovering close to Lepeka, ready to play St. George to Julian's dragon. I thought he was behaving like a clumsy old fool—abandoning his upbringing, especially in the way he had left Mrs. Warrington.

"Mrs. Warrington is leaving," I announced coolly.

"Ah! Weah you been, Sonny?" Lepeka's green eyes were filled with gloating.

"So she's leaving!" Fred's mood of the early evening was gone.

Some of the older cowboys had gathered to form a guard of honor around Mrs. Warrington, a last flourish of ceremony. One of them whisked Fred away. Julian, finely dressed in the local paniolo style, swept past us, ignoring my silent plea to be recognized. As he passed, he flashed a gorgeous look at Lepeka: bold, quick, rich in charm, and of clear intent. Her maka lea eyes flared instantaneously; a gentle smile formed of melancholy anticipation.

As soon as the ranching elite walked out, the orchestra opened with a great local favorite: *Blue Moon*. I stayed near Lepeka and her sisters, and was giving half an ear to the gossip, when someone jabbed me in the ribs from behind. I turned around, annoyed. It was Julian.

"How you, Markie? You come to da dance, too? You not too young?" His smile was dazzling.

"It's good to see you, Julian."

"How you been? You write me you ride hoss plenny time."

"I have." My eyes kept a nervous bird's watch on the front entrance.

Lepeka looked several times in our direction, determined to win again one of Julian's flashing, rutting glances. Like a skilled lover, he withheld his male largesse. She seemed undaunted.

"How iss my Puna, my one an' onny Puna?"

"He's fine now. He was pretty bad for a while."

Julian's look was serious. "Eef anyting happen to Puna, I die too!" He babbled, seemingly on the verge of tears, but pulled himself up: "Excuse me, Markie. I go see diss wahine ehu ovah heah!"

After a few exchanges in Hawaiian, Lepeka and Julian joined the dancers moving to *Blue Moon*. Bobby Ahlo's voice was good; his styling, passable. I rushed for the entrance and saw Mercedes Kaia and Piilani Launui in busy conference, heads melodramatically close. Bobby Ahlo gave a Russ Colombo twist to some of his phrasings. The song fixed itself firmly into the folds of the cool dampish night. A light fog had settled over the region.

From my perch near the front door on the verandah, I watched the intrepid dowager and her company crowd themselves into the five or six limousines that had brought them. Fred and the others in the paniolo guard of honor hovered close by and fussily assisted the chauffeurs. Island people like to travel in herds, and I have the sustained image of great aunts and uncles and their assorted acquaintances laboriously being crammed into the back seats of limousines after a concert, a poi supper, or a simple evening's call. I am there, hovering nearby—as Fred and the cowboys were that night—a fragment of the image, waiting, waiting, while Uncle Ernest or Uncle Beau, or Auntie B or Great-aunt Caroline, or the three old maid Arlington sisters, or the Princess Kahanu, or Prince Jonah, are being stuffed into waiting Buicks, La Salles, Pierce-Arrows, Packards, and a stray Daimler or Rolls Royce.

I hoped that *Blue Moon* would actually come to an end, and Lepeka would be safe in the fold of her beautiful sisters when Fred returned. But because it was the first dance tune played in more than an hour,

Bobby Ahlo kept the choruses flowing endlessly, each louder than the last. The dancers clung tighter and gave themselves up hypnotically to the unhurried motion and the magnetism of their contact. Julian and Lepeka were in a close embrace, their cheeks touching, their movements serene. A pagan air, lingering on from earlier days, seemed to surround us. We had stepped out of time, were really phantoms skittering perilously close to the outer edges of reality in our play. I wanted to leave the scene, shake off its cloying grasp, and rush down to Kawaihae to be carried home to the comforting banalities of life in Honolulu.

Fred was at the entrance. "Watching the big shots leave! You are a maha oe kid, Markie!" His voice was rasping and mean. He swept into the hall.

I had said nothing to warn him. Stray couples, seeking the night's coolness, idled near me intent on their wooing. I saw Joe coming up the steps from the lawn.

"Go and watch Uncle Fred," I said. "Lepeka is dancing with Julian."

He flew inside. The infernal repetitions of *Blue Moon* ended. There was a buzzing within the hall. To my surprise, Fred came out onto the verandah, wearing his Stetson.

"Get in the car, Mark! We're going home!" He stamped angrily toward the Packard, the fern leaves in his lei shimmering in the wan light of the lamps standing at intervals along the walkway.

I was so relieved I was crying. Joe was at my side. "Watch Julian," I blubbered. "He doesn't know what he's doing!"

"I watch heem! No worry! He O.K. You take cay-ah you cah-seen."

"That damned woman is a pain in the neck!" I wailed and ran to join Fred.

As we drove home, Fred swore hotly into the cool night air. "The woman's a Goddamned whore of Babylon! She's been a *paahau,* a prisoner, *a pipi pini,* a yoked oxen, for too damned long! Why all she wants to do now is throw her ass to the four winds!"

"You really like her a lot, Uncle Fred, and you've been good friends for a long time!"

"Not after tonight!" His voice cracked at its highest soprano. "She showed she's a real *maka lalau,* a flirt!"

I could have told Fred this from the first day she appeared at his house. Lovers are too often blinded by their own passion, I remember thinking. I had found that somewhere in my reading.

"Don't you think Julian asked Lepeka just to get your goat?"

"She should have kept her ass off that dance floor until I came back into the hall! She knew I had to do my duty by Mrs. Warrington!"

After he'd swallowed two or three half-tumblerfuls of okolehao at home, he recalled again how Lepeka had been cooped up for so many years taking care of her poor parents while her sisters had run off and found husbands, had had children, and made homes for themselves. "Women who've been penned up for so Goddamned long go nuts when a man looks at them!" Such a beautiful woman, held captive by circumstance for so long! "I should kill that black son-of-a-bitch! I'm damn near sixty years old, but they're still a few good punches left in me. I was helpless to do anything about it tonight. I have a position here to keep up! The day will come, though!" He was shrieking.

"Are you still going to give the luau?"

"My God, Markie, you're damned right, I'm going to! Laura and Louise can help me all I need. It's to celebrate my kid's birthday, ain't it? I've already invited half the people around here!"

I should have spent the rest of the night reflecting on what had happened, but once swaddled in my pajamas and dressing gown, I got under Great-aunt Louise's needlework quilt and fell quickly into a deep sleep that was infused, helter-skelter, with the happiest of dreams.

Joe came in late for breakfast with a bad hangover.

"Well, that's what you get for drinking too much! He inu lama oe, paha?" I said.

I had only jokingly called him an alcoholic, but he was dispirited the way Hawaiians always are when the celebration is over. When I started to question him about what had happened after Fred and I left the dance, he pointed to Fred's room and suggested in a hoarse whisper that I join him later when he fed the pigs and dogs. I asked him if he was going to the Baxter's luau, just to make conversation. No Hawaiian would stay away if he had any right to feel welcome.

I retired to finish some letters, when Fred called out a greeting from his bedroom where he'd spent the morning. He was wrapped like a mummy in his kapa. "Got the weebie-jeebies."

Not so *wee*! I thought, tickled at his version of the expression, and asked perfunctorily: "Is there something I can do for you?"

"Keep the kids quiet. Get 'em outa here. Take a walk along the stream." His pale-blue eyes seemed to search nervously for spots on the ceiling.

Puna leaped up from the floor where he was playing checkers with Leihulu. "We go get oranche, Markie?"

"You see what I mean? O God, my head's about to split!" He turned on his side to give emphasis to the lament.

"We go, Markie! We go!" Leihulu was now on her feet, squealing with delight.

"Not so far as the orange grove," Fred commanded, turning back toward us.

"Where is Henalee?" I asked

"I've had him doing little things for me." Fred's eyes fretfully scanned the ceiling again. "Well, what have *you* been up to all morning?"

"First of all, I gave the kids breakfast," I answered. "I've been writing letters home."

"Tell that father of yours to forget his hemorrhoids and come up here for a week or two. We'll ride his backside all over Waimea." He giggled like a schoolgirl, choked, coughed, sat up. "He's been absolutely worthless since he developed piles." He fell back on his pillow, moving his head from side to side.

Henry came with the decanter and a pitcher of water.

Fred laughed. "I'm trying to ease off today."

There was no need to ask about the luau. Fred seemed content to stay in his four-poster for the rest of the day. I had very much wanted to catch another glimpse of Waimea people celebrating.

I left the kids a moment to meet Joe at the pigpen. I managed, over the squealing, to hear him say that Lepeka and her sisters had stayed for a while and then gone somewhere else. "I teenk dat rescal buggah Kapua Gomes went take dem to one pahty. You see heem lass night? He look like Tom Mix!" Joe bent double with laughter.

Everyone at the dance had seemed to be in costume. I asked what had happened to Julian?

"He dance wit two, tree wahines. Den he fine Mele Ignacio an' he dance wit her till da en'. She one pupule wahine use to go wit Julian befoah."

"The one he . . .?" I stopped.

"No, dat one live Waipio. Mele Ignacio ees one real goodtimer from Kona."

Joe was still keeping something from me. I helped him carry pails of slops from the cooking vats in which he had mixed commercial meal with hono-hono grass, squash, and slops. The pigs squealed louder than ever.

"Dey nevah eat since lass night."

"Then nothing more happened between Julian and Lepeka after we left?"

"Dass right! *Nutting*!" He handed me a can. "Heah, make youself useful."

Together we lifted our cans to the top of the low fence and poured them into the trough. I asked where Julian was now.

"You teenk I one mine readah?" he said with a big show of annoyance and marched away with the empty cans.

The pigs grunted and slurped lasciviously, fascinating in their animal esurience.

"Eef you like see someting, Markie, go insigh my room," Joe said in a matter-of-fact tone.

Joe's rooms, formerly the quarters of the head groom, were in the stable next to the tack room. I stopped short when I saw someone standing just inside the tack room door. Julian stepped into the open. He beckoned me. I went.

"I come las night! Dis morning, I mean!" He was disheveled and bleary-eyed; his tan gabardine trousers, wrinkled; his boots, splotched with mud. His bare torso was the color of mahogany from working on deck in swim shorts. He was very much at ease.

"He come from da field behin'," said Joe. "Dass why da ilio no bark!"

"I pound on da doah an' make him pu-iwa!"

"*An' how* he make me scay-ad!" Then in Hawaiian Joe excitedly explained how Julian, drunk, had insisted on seeing Puna before returning to Kawaihae.

We were about to enter the tack room to avoid being discovered when Georgie Punohu, the compulsive tattle-tale, came into view under the saddling shed. Too late, Julian stepped inside the tack room; he had been sighted by Georgie. I stayed outside with Joe. We tried several ways of getting rid of Georgie without giving him a chance to tell Fred, all without success. We were getting desperate, when Georgie asked where the children were.

"I'm taking them for a walk along the stream. How about joining us? Uncle Fred is asleep."

"We going to da luau."

"When?"

"Louise say foah da second sitting."

"All the kalua pig will be gone."

"When did Julian come diss place?"

"Last night. This morning. I don't know when."

Joe was anxious to get cleaned-up and be off to the luau. He slipped into the tack room, and there were fast exchanges in Hawaiian between him and Julian.

"O.K., Markie. I going home," Georgie skittered out of the saddling shed.

I caught him near the clump of ginger. "You say one word to Uncle Fred and I'll knock your block off!"

The children had clustered at the tack room door, calling me. Puna was already scrambling up the short flight of steps. Julian met him at the doorway, lifted him into his arms, and the wailing began: "My baby, my puu-wai, my heart! My precious flower, my sweet baby!" He shed tears shamelessly and clung to the child as though protecting him. Henry and Leihulu ran into the tack room and put their arms around their uncle. They were all crying.

"His heart is broke," Joe said as I came in. Julian was babbling in Hawaiian. "Eef you unnerstan' what he say, eet get you heah! Onny Hawaiians feel diss kine luff." He too was crying. Now *I* was on the brink of tears.

"You come back stay wit us, Uncle Julian?" Puna implored, sitting now on Julian's knee.

"Bime-by, baby, bime-by!" One of his large hands encompassed the side of the child's head and pulled it to his breast. "Au'we! Au'we! Eha loa ka puu wai. Na'u oe keiki aloha! Na'u oe! You are mine, keiki punahele! Mine!"

There was something too savage, too abandoned, in this show of heartbreak. I was in great conflict, but unconscious forces prevailed, and I began to shed tears of wrath or sympathy. Even my parents would have looked upon this as being "too Hawaiian." That day in Waimea I shed tears without shame, even as I attempted to look at what was happening from the perspective of the judge, the British Earl, and the American missionary, my haole ancestors.

"Come back *now*! Come back *now,* Uncle!" Puna begged.

Julian answered through broken sobs: "I got one job now, keiki, on da boat—da *beeg* boat!"

"Boat?" the child appealed, diverted now.

"Da cattle boat, da *Moi.* Da *King!*"

"You like da boat, Uncle?" Leihulu wanted to know.

"An' how you like Honolulu?" asked Henry.

"No can beat Waimea! Waimea no ka oi!"

The tears dried on the cheeks over which a short time ago they had flowed like cascades down a mountainside. Julian and the children were laughing and teasing one another. I was shocked that I had not appreciated the degree of affection between them.

The first loud crack from the kitchen porch brought back the pig hunt. It sounded again. Unmistakably, Fred was at work with his bull whip!

"Puppa!" the children shrieked.

"Quick, Julian! You must get out of here!" I took Puna from him.

"Dis time I no run," he growled. "Where Joe put his bull-wheep?" He searched frantically, muttering words I could not understand. The children cried. I pleaded. Fred shrieked oaths in Hawaiian as loud as a sugar refinery whistle. Henry and Leihulu ran to their father. Puna clung to me, trembling.

"My uncle is deadly with that whip!" I said to Julian.

"Doan worry! Cool head da main ting!"

I almost smiled.

Fred was approaching, Leihulu and Henry clinging to his legs like squid, making it difficult for him to crack the whip again. Finally he shook Leihulu to the ground, her long hair sweeping the dry earth of the saddling shed and gathering bits of horse excrement. When Henry was flung loose, we could see that Fred had dressed hurriedly. He was barefoot and wore last night's white cashmere breeches slipped on over his cotton longies.

"Come out of there, Markie!" I held my ground. "I said to come outa there, you Goddamned little smart aleck from Honolulu!"

"Use your whip on me, Uncle Fred. I'm not afraid!"

Puna trembled violently. Leihulu, on her feet again, tried to smooth her hair, using both hands as combs.

Fred came for me. Julian pushed me aside, flew out the door, and landed on Fred with his full weight. He had found a whip. Fred rolled to one side and unseated Julian who leaped outside the saddling shed. Fred's whip on Julian's bare back would break the skin. I rushed into Joe's room, found a jacket, and threw it out. Julian ignored it. Damned ass! I thought.

"Take the churrens away, Markie!" Julian breathed hard.

Fred, arms bent, body at a slight slant, readied himself for the attack; his whip, unfurled; its tip slipping over glistening tufts of grass like an eel in a seaweed bed. It cracked like a gunshot.

Julian jumped high. Fred had merely been warming up. Julian snapped his whip, no match for Fred. I told Leihulu to take Puna next door, but Puna refused to let loose. Henry ran to the bath house to get Joe. Puna had the hold of a drowning swimmer.

As I screamed "Julian! Grab the whip!" it caught him on the shoulder. He leaped forward, aimed low in a sidewise thrust, and caught Fred full around the waist. Julian pulled hard, but Fred inserted a thumb and broke the hold. He lunged heavily toward Julian again, snapping his whip in quick, short thrusts, but the younger man was too agile.

"Coupla bloody stupid heads," Joe grumbled coming up, and laid his towel and shaving gear carefully on the grass.

Julian caught Fred again, around the ass. Fred screeched in pain. "Black pig!"

Puna wailed to the limits of his vocal chords. Fred coiled his whip around Julian's neck like a noose. Julian jerked the butt from Fred's hands and was on the older man, pounding him with fists like sledge-hammers. Fred fell.

Joe rushed toward the two men. I peeled the hysterical Puna away from my legs and gave him to Henry, who was frozen into a shriveled image of himself. Joe and I pulled Julian away. Both men were wounded.

"I geev you dat foah my sistah, foah dese

churrens, and foah all da uddah peepuls you hana-ino!" Julian looked like a kahuna of Kamehameha's time, cursing and infuriating the sharks in Kawaihae Bay from the walls of Puu Kohola Heiau.

"Get out of here, Julian!" I ordered, frenzied. "There's been enough trouble!"

"I go wit pleasure!" he said throatily. His eyes slowly scanned the surroundings, searching, I thought, for Puna.

I bent down to help Fred.

"I'm okay, boy. A little pi-ula. Get me a towel to wipe my nose. Look at all this blood," he chortled. Then he shrieked: "Why that laho pilau! He ia ule palaho!"

"Uncle Fred, there's been enough name calling."

A wave of ylang-ylang fragrance passed over us from the huge viny mass near the lower boundary of the yard, almost sickening me. Henry helped me walk the groaning Fred to the drinking trough under the pomelo tree.

"Where's Puna?" I asked, surprised he wasn't with Henry.

The cousins from next door arrived en masse. Louise had her usual calm and glowing health, but Laura was deathly pale. Their visiting brother, Bill Punohu, was of average height but built like a bull. Georgie lurked close to his side looking intermittently repentant and triumphant. I was sure he had somehow managed to tell Fred that Julian was on the property. Bill's wife, a beautiful Chinese woman with a child in her arms, brought up the rear.

"There are evil things in the air, Cousin Fred. Evil things!" Laura made faint gasps between each word. "Miriam Lono has been coming to me. She wants her child."

Fred lifted his red face out of the water in the trough, his mustaches dripping streams of water down onto his undershirt. His voice was ear-splitting. Laura babbled and then fainted, falling toward her brother Bill.

Fred stomped into the house, saying, "The gall of that woman. Kind of nonsense! Spiritualism! Cannibalism! Communism! Kahunaism!"

Laura's resuscitation caused another stir. She was a wraith as pale as moonlight. She said things that were imperceptible.

"Somebody get water," Bill Punohu ordered. I brought a pitcher and glass from the kitchen. Gently, Bill placed the rim between his sister's thin gray lips. She sipped daintily.

The urgent need to find Puna gave me an excuse to escape. I checked Fred's room, Joe's, and the secondary buildings. I went down to the stream, walked up it for a half-mile or so, peering into the thickets of ginger, fern, and guava along its banks. Henry at some point had decided to follow me. We met as I cut back downstream.

"You nevah fine Puna?" he sing-songed in pidgin.

"Did you check all over the house?"

"I went upstairs. I went in Gramma's bedroom."

"Where's Leihulu?"

"Aunty Louise tole her foah go home wit dem. She was scare somting else might happen."

"Maybe Puna followed them."

"No."

We leaped from rock to rock, making a game of our disquieting mission. I noticed that the water in the stream here was clearer, the algae discolorations yellowish, different from Oahu streams. We came to a place in the stream where watercress grew.

"Let's pick some for supper," I proposed.

"I hate le-koa. Is beetah an' hot!" Henry reached down for handfuls of strands of greens. "We nevah eat so much, Markie, till you come." He made up two bundles, using strips of a crushed ginger stalk as ties.

We crossed the short stretch of field that separated the stable from the stream. The tousled tops of eucalyptus growing near the stream swayed perilously close to the snapping point under the trade wind gusts. Goats bleated warnings as we approached the stable.

"Brutes!" I muttered.

"You no like goats?"

"At times they seem to be real proud bastards."

"Goats is goats! How dey can be proud?"

I didn't like it when Fred called sows and bitches "whores," dogs "gangsters," and horses "Fancy Dans." But I hadn't been as truthful and courageous as Henry.

"Did you look in Uncle Julian's room?" I asked suddenly and ran as fast as I could toward Uncle Palani's porch. The door was unlocked. Lepeka had been using the room for storage: boxes of pheasant skins, half-stuffed birds, boars' heads, jars of formaldehyde, and broken pieces of furniture.

Puna was asleep behind a bureau set criss-cross in a corner, curled up like a bear cub in its first wintery sleep. I woke him gently, lifting him to his feet. He began to whimper.

"It's all right, Puna. It's all right. I'm Markie! We've been looking all over for you. Don't cry."

"Puppa fight wit Uncle Julian! Uncle Julian hit Puppa wit da whip! Puppa hit him back!" he sobbed.

"It's all over now. It's all over. Puppa is asleep. I'll make you a sandwich or French toast."

The child seemed unable to stop sobbing.

Puna wolfed down a part of each sandwich and fell into a listlessness, a disinterest. He stared idly across the table, out the windows next to the kitchen door. I sat there, watching him, saying things that failed to win his interest.

I did not hear the car nor the barking dogs. Kapua Gomes had brought Lepeka and her sisters, all dressed in holokus and leis, all of them a little tight.

They were alarmed by Fred's battered face. Mary Ann asked point-blank, "Who beat you up?" By her sly look I knew they already knew of the fight; half of Waimea would have known thanks to Georgie, but Fred replied with unusual calm that he'd had a bad fall last night, wandering around the yard. "I got dead-drunk." He looked reproachfully at Lepeka. She responded with cajoling and whimpering: "So surprise when I foun' out you leaf da dance hall." One sister made a flattering comment about the house to dispel the mood. Fred chuckled agreeably about how difficult it was for a wifeless man to maintain such a place and offered to show the house to Mary Ann and Mercedes. "A drink first!" he cackled like an aroused guinea fowl.

Plans for the luau were discussed for an hour with typical Hawaiian monotony. Hawaiians love to repeat, as in chant. They lull themselves into states of repose built on endless repetition by beautiful voices. Kapua Gomes would drone: "Moluhi an' I go gat da maile! We gat da maile foah da leis! No worry, Fred, Moluhi an' we gat da maile foah da leis. No worry! No worry!" Then he would repeat this in Hawaiian, like an undersong at the altar of Laka, goddess of the hula, propitiated with woodland blossoms and greenery, especially the fragrant maile vine.

They discussed varieties of limu and raw fish, the amount of taro leaves needed to cook with chicken or squid, and decided who should make the starchy coconut puddings: kulolo and haupia. Someone boldly suggested hiring professional musicians. Fred balked. The bold one insisted. Fred capitulated. Honey Smithers and her troup, the most popular voice and string ensemble in the island, would be summoned from Hilo. Piilani offered to call Honey Smithers when she went to Honoka'a in a day or two. She also offered the services of her husband, Ikuwa, to help prepare the cook the pigs. He was known in the region for his expertise. Mercedes offered to go to Kona to buy a lau of fish, a lau of squid. "We'll have pulehu squid, raw squid, and squid with luau!"—referring, lastly, to the tenderest leaves of taro which bears the same name as the Hawaiian feast. Lepeka reminded her sisters that a luau was paa hapa, half-complete, without opae kuahiwi, the sweet little fresh-water shrimps that abounded in the mountain streams of Kohala. In a chorus, all agreed to go to Kohala a day or two before the luau to gather opae and the leaf buds of fern served with this delicacy.

Waves of laughter penetrated the house. Anticipation of the luau brought the women close to euphoria. The enjoyment begins for Hawaiians from the first moment of the planning stage. Sunken spirits, sore arms, legs, and backs, are noticed only after the last tipsy guest has taken his leave.

The women and Gomes left before dark. Fred retired to his father's porch after dinner with his concertina. He sang a few songs and patiently and tenderly explained their origin and meaning to the children. Puna sat on the steps, not at his father's feet, and stared into the darkness. I went to sit by him, but he kept his silence, and I moved away.

Fred stood, stretched, yawned, belched a few times. "Some days are not worth living, boy," he said to me.

"I know what you mean, Uncle Fred."

The night's silence engulfed us. I was seized by a great lassitude.

"C'mon, you kids, it's time for bed. You can bathe in Mumma's bathroom tonight. You go first, Leihulu."

Puna lingered near me.

"Aren't you going in, Puna?"

"Yup!" He rushed to me, planted a kiss on my cheek, and scurried into the bedroom after his father and the other children.

I leaned on the railing and lifted my eyes to the sky, now filled with pale yellow stars. I half-heard myself say, "Please, you up there, whatever you are, whoever you are, help us."

The forty-foot long luau tent Fred had wormed from Albert Baxter was lifted above the lawn between the stone wall and the kitchen garden. Joe and two of his cousins from Kona had woven a truckload of coconut fronds into screens to hide "unsightly areas": the dog houses, the outdoor toilet, and the place where we prepared food for the animals.

Three tables of one-by-twelves laid across wooden sawhorses ran the length of the tent. Wrapping paper covered the planks, and over the paper a thick layer of ferns—fragrant lau'ae and lacy palapalai—was spread, with roses, pansies, lilies and soda pop bottles, splashing color like Bonnard brush strokes.

Strands of maile were wound around the tent poles and the railing of the platform for the Honey Smithers Troupe at the far end of the tent, facing the house. The side flaps of the tent were rolled up, revealing the heavy plantings inside the stone wall; kiss-me-quick, pakalana, gardenia, and magnolia were in the heaviest bloom of the summer. The fragrances of the ferns and flowers mingled with the smoky odor of the imu-roasted pig and the fruity bouquet of okolehao: island smells, heavy, compelling, at times overpowering.

The pigs had been swilled at noon with prodigious amounts of food to keep them quiet through the afternoon and evening. The dogs were tethered behind the bath house.

Puna was dressed as a miniature cowboy in new boots, tightfitting gabardine trousers and matching jacket: a junior member of that proud Waimea order of men who, for more than a hundred and twenty years, had tended the great herds of the Stevenson Ranch.

Laura and Louise had made a new dress for Leihulu in the past week, fearing that Uncle Fred would pay little attention to her. Lepeka had taken great pains, combing and brushing Leihulu's luxuriant hair.

"I no like da ribbon, Aunty!" Leihulu complained.

"Bime-bye you takum off eef you like! . . . Aftah we pau eat."

The child pecked Lepeka's cheek and raced off to the cousins next door to give them a private showing of the stunning dress. Louise and Laura would not attend the luau. Laura was feeling poorly.

Others would not be coming. Dr. Jake Brown and his wife were going to be in Hilo; Ben, Fred had told me, would probably not come. "He won't go anywhere that woman of his is not wanted. She's very backward, and on top of that, she's toothless. I'll send a pu-olu of food up to Ben. Lord alive, I don't want to cut off my son from all our affairs, just because he's got a Jap common-law wife." This was news to me.

Muscular Portuguese ranchers, some of whom leased lands from Fred, came from the Hamakua Coast, with their wives and husky children, heaped with gifts of food: links of blood and pork sausage, sweet bread, baked in igloo-shaped stone ovens in their back yards. Japanese vegetable farmers arrived in large family groups: their wives saying little, smiling happily; their children, bewitching. The parents bowed deeply, presenting meticulously packaged homemade gifts for Puna: a little padded Japanese dressing jacket, hand-sewn cotton zabutons, and cleverly designed wooden toys. Leihulu was remembered with a hand-fashioned Japanese doll; and Henry with an elephant puzzle of interlocking pieces of wood, which I never succeeded in reassembling, although Henry did. Satoru Moriyama presented Fred with a shaped bonsai of a lehua tree, planted when he first settled in the remote, heavily wooded section of Puukapu to tend the great ditch that brought water from the Kohala Mountains to the Waimea region.

Mrs. Warrington—in the expansive way of islanders—delighted Fred by bringing people he had not invited because they lived so far from Waimea. They had joined their limousines to Mrs. Warrington's caravan at different stages of its progress. Hapa-haoles of the old ranching families of the monarchy met infrequently now under one roof.

"This is a typical old-time luau!" Mrs. Warrington said, during the feasting.

"Pololei keia!" Emma Pittman replied. She was the elder of the tall, hapa-haole "old maid Pittman sisters" who managed their own ranch on the Kona Coast. When young, they had ridden out every day with the paniolos. They lived in a sprawling house that overlooked the entire coastline, whence they offered hospitality on a lavish scale to a small circle of friends.

Outside the front stone wall, thirty or forty saddle horses snorted and stamped in the grassy roadside shoulder across from the row of limousines. The chauffeurs joined the guests. In the days of the monarchy, members of the royal family often gave luaus to which the whole town was invited.

The Honey Smithers Troupe sang popular Hawaiian tunes and songs related specifically to Waimea persons or places. Honey Smithers, over six feet tall and heavy, danced, much to the amusement of everyone, a new hapa-haole tune written for a movie idol: *The Cock-eyed Mayor of Kaunakakai.* Fred and some of the cowboys hurled risque references in Hawaiian to her great opu, ample breasts, and monumental backside. Honey absorbed these as compliments, and, swaying her hips first in one direction, then another, tossed them back—haughty, disdainful, erotic—at her taunting admirers.

Two younger women danced to the words of Prince Peter Kaeo's chant: *Hiilawe.* Aunt Bella Naihe translated for me and explained how the song extolled the beauty of a waterfall in Waipio Valley which the prince had visited with his adored cousin, the late Queen Emma Kaleleonalani, and had recalled later when a patient at the Molokai leper colony.

"Pita is writing about Emma when he tells of the beauty and grace of Hiilawe. Ui loa a pau keia mele! It is a very beautiful mele, indeed!"

Lepea danced in the nineteenth century native style: bent knees, uplifted heels: the position of the hula olapa; her movements meaningful, even thrilling. Never before had I seen the hula danced in this spirited, primitive way. Fred sat through her first hula, stony-faced. In the old families it was often remarked: "We have the hula performed for us—we do not dance it." Lepeka had grown up unaffected in her lively movements: swaying arms, feet kneading the earth or floor, hips gyrating.

"She's good! She's very good!" Mrs. Warrington said with a broad smile and toss of her head. "That's the way it was danced when the missionaries weren't looking!"

Aunt Hannah Shipley replied simply, "Oiaio no!" She was a woman of sensitivity and some learning, described often as "a great reader of books."

Her portly son Gresham Shipley drank prodigiously all afternoon but carried his load "like a mountain with a sparrow on its shoulder," as Robert Louis Stevenson described King Kalakaua imbibing. Shipley showered Fred with questions about cattle and horses. They were joined by tall young Hartley Baxter, whose blond hair and pale skin advertised the fact that the Baxters and the Hartleys were among the old haole families which had not mixed their bloods. Uncle Peyton Russell came over, drawing his cousin, Judge Henry Peyton. I loitered at the edge of the group.

"Well, if you think we'll ever get far here with herds of Santa Gertrudis, you're quite mistaken," Uncle Peyton Russell argued.

"Has anyone planted substantial amounts of the new African grass?" young Baxter asked.

Now Eben Dinwiddie was at my side. "Shop talk! Just my meat!" He listened earnestly.

As they talked, the older men directed glances at Eben which were both pedagogic and deferential. I looked at him with envy and admiration. Judge Peyton was saying something about recessive traits. I was avidly interested in genealogies and would listen patiently to lengthy, complex discussions of the subject, willing to offer a clarifying date or name, if asked to participate; but when it came to pedigrees, I was easily lost. I walked away toward the stables.

Halfway there I ran into Albert Baxter, who had been viewing Fred's various enterprises. I was aware for the first time of his towering size. Like his son, his face was pinkish, his eyes a watery blue. His peppery gray mustache was not as flamboyant as Fred's.

"Walking off all that rich Hawaiian food, eh, boy?" His smile belied my assumption that he would always wear a look of austere preeminence. "That's just what I've been doing."

There was an awkward silence. I was itching to talk with this legendary nabob, this living image of successful ranching, who might once have taken charge of our ranches and made them as successful as this one, had it not been for . . . what? Family bickering? A better offer? Or something more personal? I had not accepted Fred's explanation.

"I know a number of the Hulls. I went to school with Albert . . . also with Beaufort Hull. I knew Edward and Willson . . . and Sybil. Lord, what a beauty she was! There was another Hull girl. Married a fella from Shanghai. I believe they went to England to live?"

"That was my grand-aunt, Eudora. Eudora Hull Stanhope."

"Of course! My goodness, the Hulls are such a huge clan. Now, with the new crop, I imagine that you find it hard to keep track of everyone, even among yourselves."

I studied the man's face, his imposing frame, his large hands. At times I could be so absorbed that my scrutiny veered toward rudeness. I could not help myself. I saw fellow humans as aesthetic objects, as repositories of music, art, poetry—of elements similar to ones I found in a view of the sky, the sea, or the mountains.

"I knew your father when he was a kid riding with the cowboys out at Makuakai. He used to ride Ed Hull's race horses at Kapiolani."

"In the gentleman riders' race. My father was too big to be a jockey."

"Tell me, young fella, what is your father doing? Does he keep any stock?"

"He works in the land office. He's a searcher of titles. We are no longer landowners." Everyone in the islands knew of the sordid transactions that had led to the destruction of the Hull Estate lands.

The big man felt my indignation. "Your father would have made a fine rancher. It was in his blood."

"Is it true that you were once approached by my great-grandfather to manage our ranches?"

"That was a long, long time ago, my boy." He seemed massively of a mind not to enlarge on the subject.

"What happened, Mr. Baxter?" I asked with some humility.

"I was quite young—home from college for only a few years. That was in 1896—just after the Queen's supporters attempted to overthrow the provisional government. Your people were Royalist to the core. My own family was split down the middle. I was on the side of the P.G.'s—that is, not a Royalist."

"One of your brothers was killed," I blurted.

"It was a terrible blow. My Uncle, David O. Baxter, on the other hand, was a staunch Royalist. As a matter of fact, he was the Queen's business agent."

This detail of Baxteriana jarred the traditional view I'd always received from my family.

"You can imagine what talk took place in our family gatherings! My father, whose people had come here from England when he was a boy, was also a Royalist. My mother's people were mikanele . . . Do you know what that means?"

"Missionary."

"My mother was on the side of the reformers."

"A house divided against itself . . . It was my father's phrase when he met opposition from my mother."

Baxter laughed for the first time. "What a fiasco that whole thing was. When I think of it now, I sometimes feel embarrassed. Now to get back to your people," he said, rubbing his mustache. "Edward was very much in favor of my taking over their ranches. Willson was not. They had disagreed for years."

"Uncle Willson did things the old-fashioned way. Uncle Edward had been trained in California and England."

Baxter's eyes were friendly. "They hated one another! I heard that Edward had caused the death of Willson's finest breeding stallion in some careless mix-up, and *that* was really the cause."

"I've heard about that damned stallion all my life! His name was Kepalo! Devil!"

Mr. Baxter grinned. "Willson Hull is a funny man! He's deep! I try to see him sometimes when I go to town."

"He is a very emotional man, on the primitive side, but I like him. They say Uncle Edward was prayed to death by a kahuna. He'd cut the lip of a paniolo's son who had thrown a rock at my cousin Columbus Hull that made a big gash on the side of his face."

I had the sickening feeling I had said too much.

"I hope, my boy, you don't believe that nonsense! Edward Hull was as white as the rest of us! As white as you are! Don't let yourself be taken in by that nonsense! It's destructive! And, if I were you, my boy, I wouldn't repeat that story. Why, if I'm not mistaken, your family is Episcopalian, among Bishop Staley's first parishioners!"

"I was confirmed two years ago, and I have never told that story to anyone but you. Not even to my cousin, Fred Andrews."

"That's good!" he smiled approvingly.

"There were many arguments then about your managing our ranches?"

"Good Lord! How that old paakiki mule, Willson Hull, balked. He demanded this exclusion, that exclusion! Hell! He wanted to keep Manulani for himself! Eddie thought one management would be more productive. He also thought it would reduce family differences to give the management to an outsider. When there's too much huki-huki, it's best to let a neutral party step in."

"My father says Uncle Willson raised the most beautiful Arabian horses anyone ever saw here!"

"But he didn't make enough money to justify the use of all that land." Mr. Baxter turned to see what was happening under the tent. Cake and coffee were being served. "I must say, young fella, you know one hell of a lot about the old days. Most kids your age don't seem to care! I'd better be getting back to Mrs. Baxter. We're having the twins and that ranching crowd their grandmother gathered up last week to dinner tonight." He fell silent, and then decided to speak: "I hated to let the old man Hull down, my boy. He knew I regarded the Hull lands in terms of their economic value—in terms of their being profitable ranches. I was not so personally attached. George Hull was a truly good man, and capable—like some of the chiefs of olden times."

"Just about that time, Sam Dawson offered you the management of all this!"

"I thank God every day that he did. We've had a wonderful life here!"

I was glowing with our conversation.

"Let me tell you one thing, my boy. All we've been talking about is far behind us now. It's pau! It's dead! Don't dwell on it. You can eat your heart out thinking about it." I nodded. "I can tell you one thing. If you live up to the promise you show now, you'll certainly amount to something. I've had one hell of a good time talking to you, son."

He sauntered off, a haole alii, a chief of today. I walked slowly toward the stable to see the imu, the pit in which the pig had been kalua-ed. The pit was still smoking, surrounded by the mound of earth excavated in the digging. The smell of cooked flesh and leaves of ti and banana hovered everywhere. Paniolos were strumming their ukuleles, singing or talking. They had abandoned the tent to the gentry, once the feast was over.

I met Dr. Okamura and his wife Moira walking up from the stream.

"The smell of the imu is very strong," I said as we approached the pit.

"Always concern' 'bout smells, Markie! How you been?"

"Have you seen Puna?" I asked.

Puna had sat through the luau with Fred at the head of the table, his dark eyes empty, perhaps bored. Mrs. Warrington had remarked to me: "Your little cousin is not well, or he's very unhappy about something. It makes me anu-e to look at him."

"He seemed preoccupied, a little lissless," said Dr. Okamura, "but dat may be da excitement."

"Children shrink into themselves when something overwhelms them," Moira added.

I told them how Puna had been acting recently.

"When you have da chance, bring him to your room, Markie."

Eben Dinwiddie joined us. I performed the introductions; then the Okamuras left us together.

"His wife is a beauty," said Eben. His eyes scanned the surroundings. "My grandmother told me this was once quite a place."

We explored and found, to my surprise, the Andrews' burial ground just beyond the side gate to Aunt Millie's long-uninhabited cottage. A large tombstone rose in the middle, surrounded by smaller ones. Clumps of kiss-me-quick shielded the place from the highway.

"Life is funny," I said, feeling giddy. I would not let myself slip into melancholy.

We walked back to the house. Huge pots were being washed in the kitchen, piles of dishes were being scraped, and pu-olus of food were being made up for certain of the guests to take home. In the breakfast room, several of Gerta's gorgeous cakes remained untouched on the oak table. I pointed to the masterpiece that had so stymied me.

"*Kroa, The Ape Boy*," Eben said. Then he howled. I had to grab a chair as I doubled over with laughter.

"We had one of those little monsters, too," Eben said finally. "Used to scare the pants off us. My great-grandparents went to that same exposition in Paris. They took old Palani, I think." We laughed uncontrollably.

"Come on," I said when we had regained our composure. We entered the parlor.

"Like a suite we had once at the Hotel Meurice in Paris," he said soberly. There's a big trunk full of portraits in the little house my great-great-grandfather built at Puumalu—old Lemuel, the first. I'd like to get them out some day and hang them."

"I like old pictures, but they make me sad."

"They should make you happy. They show what people looked like—what a place was like."

"That's the trouble. They remind you that people die. That places fall apart, or burn down."

"What's wrong with that?"

Upstairs, Eben went immediately to the great round marble-topped table. "Was this old Palani's gaming table? A fantastic place, this! No wonder my grandmother and the other old-timers talk about it so much. Last night at dinner they were all talking about Aunt Louise and Uncle Palani. They were very important people in their time."

"We might have been related," I ventured.

"My Great-uncle Tony . . ."

". . . was engaged to Sybil Hull," I finished. "I think you take after him some. Aunt Sybil showed me several pictures of him."

Eben ran a brown hand over the smooth marble surface of the table. "We're leaving for Honolulu on Tuesday. I'm afraid we won't have our ride."

"You won't be here when the stallion arrives?"

He grinned, his white teeth flashing. "No can help! C'est la vie!"

"Do you like living away from here?"

"Locked up in hotel rooms? Being pushed around in the streets, bundled up like a mummy? Lemuel likes the theater. *This* is my world!" His right arm cut an arc through the air. "I know just the spot where I want to build my own house! I'm fed up with the old homes cluttered together here."

In one of the little north bedrooms, we found Puna curled up asleep, his maile and rose leis tangled under his chin, forming a pillow.

"What's this little birthday guy doing up here?" Eben asked, surprised.

We went down the flight of stairs, I, holding Puna by the hand. Puna droned all the way to my bedroom: "I like sleep! I like sleep!" I began to remove his crushed leis and unbutton his jacket. He fussed irritably. "Dr. Okamura wants to see you, Puna."

"I not sick!"

"He only wants to give you a quick check-up."

"Do you think anyone would mind if I tried playing on that little organ in the parlor?" Eben asked. I heard the reedy sputterings of *Aloha Oe* as Eben's fingers sought out the keys.

Dr. Okamura sounded Puna's thorax repeatedly for the least sign of pleurisy.

"His temperature is normal, pulse is good. There seems to be nothing wrong in his chess. I would say he was doing fine. How's his appetite?"

"Not so good," I said.

"What do you mean by that, Markie!" Fred snapped. "He ate two dishes of kalua pig, three sweet potatoes, and a big dish of lomi salmon today."

"I think he looks a little tired," Moira Okamura suggested. "Maybe he should be put to bed early. Children get low-spirited when their resistance is down. They need sympathy, attention."

Fred ignored the implied criticism.

"We'll say goodbye now, Mr. Andrews," the doctor said. "It was a great party!"

"I don't know when I've been so moved. It was all so exotic!" his wife joined in.

"The doctor saved my boy's life!" Fred's statement was sincere and open.

Later, Mrs. Warrington and I found a place to talk.

"I can't tell you how much I've enjoyed our chats, Mark. How sweet it is sometimes to talk about the old days. You've brought back so many memories . . . Elsie Hull, your grandfather, Fred's mother, Louise . . ." She looked at me with a clear gaze. "Uncle Tony and Aunt Sybil! My word, what a courtship that was. I only heard about it—I was a bit younger than Sybil. Lemuel began courting me a few years later. I spent last week with my grandsons, circling the island. Look at the mob I collected—the Shipleys, the Pittman girls, Lucy and Peyton Russell. It's a revelation to come back to Hawaii."

They were leaving Waimea on Tuesday. "We haven't decided yet whether to go back to Paris or stay in New York. The boys' tutors will be disappointed if we don't go back. I got a young Frenchman fresh from the Sorbonne to teach them archaeology and the other sciences, and an older man, an Englishman, to drum literature and history into their heads. He's an Oxford man—Magdelen. My last husband was English, a barrister. He was at New College. Do you know my sister Rena's husband, Bert Constable? He worked for a time at the Bodleian. Rena met him in

England when she was visiting Princess Kaiulani. Talk to Bert, if you want to go to Oxford."

I said, "I thought I'd go to Harvard."

"The main thing is to go to college." She looked around as though to catch someone's eye. "Well, young Mark, it's time I gathered up the stray kittens and went home. The Baxters are giving us dinner tonight. *Dinner*! I don't even want to *think* of food for the next week. Too bad, really! Old Pang Kui makes the best fresh coconut pie."

I sat on Uncle Palani's porch alone, waiting for Fred's return. He had taken Lepeka home, both of them well in their cups.

A fire still burned in the imu, and near it Joe had lit the paper cups and other debris gathered from around the tent. The smoke filled the moist night air. It was the one thing about a luau that I thoroughly disliked: the odor of wilted flowers and leaves and burning fat-soaked debris, when you are glutted with rich fare.

The big tent was a dim rectangular mass: more a tomb than a shelter for feasting people; musicians and dancers; the buzz of talk, the bursts of laughter and singing.

Puna had not wakened since I'd taken him to his room. I felt suddenly a strong need to talk to my parents. Fred could not give me the comfort of an adult. Mrs. Warrington had been supportive, but her glow of heart, her stern, strong, loving, clear-headed responses belonged to Eben and Lemuel Gaylord—not to me!

Fred had nearly reached the porch before I noticed him.

"Shill up, boy? I got good newsh to tell you!" He was on the porch. He plopped himself into a wicker chair. "You are the firsh one to be told in thish houshhold, Markie!" He slapped his knees, laughing sardonically. "I'm going to marry Lepeka on Friday necks. Take time off tomorrow to get the lischense. Going to Waipio for Shaturday an' Shunday. You don't mind shtaying with the kidsh, Markie? Jusht think, she'll be number *four*, my boy! How'sh that for a record?"

"Aunty Lepeka is a fine woman, Uncle Fred."

"Ash fine ash they come." Rising awkwardly, he said, "Letsh have a nightcap in honor of the fifth Mishush Fred Androosh!"

I led him staggering through the bedrooms to the kitchen. A lamp was burning, but Joe and his cousins had left.

I was working a puzzle to amuse Puna in the breakfast room, when we were surprised by a knocking at the front door. Since I had been in the house, no caller had used that entrance.

Leihulu ran in breathless. "Markie! Markie! Da kine is here! Mrs. Warrington! Da man who drive her car say she like see you!"

I was hopeful that Mrs. Warrington had come with good news. What news? The chauffeur strode off ahead of me, a stately warrior. Masai? I thought. Zulu?

Mrs. Warrington sat in saintly repose, dressed all in white, in the rear seat of the limousine. "Good morning, Mark! I've come to say good-bye." She wore white gloves, her panama hat was banded with a lei of red apapane feathers. "I've brought you something. Come in the car and sit beside me."

The mouse-gray upholstery was smooth velvet; the woodwork inside the doors and back of the driver's seat was as fine as that in the Rolls Royce Aunt Eudora Hull Stanhope had brought with her from England when she paid us a visit two years before.

Puna was sitting on the garden wall.

"It's such a beautiful day!" Mrs. Warrington's eyes searched the treetops. "On days like this, Waimea is paradise." She noticed Puna. "I'd ask the little fellow to join us, but I want to talk."

"He follows me everywhere lately."

"He's grown fond of you. That's not impossible to do. Eben likes you very much, and I've been greatly impressed with how much you know about the old days. Look here!" She picked up a wooden case that resembled one for dueling pistols and opened it. "Do you know what these are?"

"They're English spurs!"

"Yes, silver spurs. They belonged to Tony—Uncle Tony Stevenson!" She removed one from the case and held it before her. "Tony was such a dude. His name is engraved on these."

"Eben looks like him, I think!"

A gray look passed over her face. Hawaiians intertwine the fates of people from one generation to the next who bear the same name or somehow resemble each other.

"I want you to have these spurs, Mark. I was keeping them for one of my grandsons, but I think, for certain reasons, they are more appropriately yours. Eben agrees with me." She returned the bright spur to its place in the plush-lined case. Her eyes were moistening. I prayed that she wouldn't make this another incident of Waimea sadness. She handed me the case. "Take them with my aloha!"

"I'll always treasure them!" I could scarcely speak.

"Of course you will," she said in a low voice.

"I feel strange having Uncle Tony Stevenson's spurs. Anu e."

Mrs. Warrington fingered her large, white beaded handbag. "If I thought it would make you uneasy . . ."

"Please don't misunderstand, Aunt Nita. Uncle Tony has meant a great deal to me. From the first time I can remember hearing about him, he's been a . . ."

"A kind of hero to you?"

"Yes. And my Aunt Sybil has always been a heroine."

"You love the past, Mark. That's obvious. It's a rare thing in a youngster nowadays. Sybil and Tony are your Romeo and Juliet . . . your Dante and Beatrice."

"So you see, I never thought I would have something of *his.*"

"What a strange boy you are. You are full of feelings." She gave me a sharp look. "You'll either be a raging success or a nervous wreck before you're thirty."

I touched the spurs carefully, as though willing them to reveal some coveted secret. I was unnerved. "Everybody talks about kahunas and their powers." I was exercising my own sense of justice. Ownership of Tony Stevenson's spurs put a new kind of burden on me.

"That's one of the reasons I've taken my grandsons away from here. All this primitive nonsense can be harmful. We don't know enough about it to make it meaningful anymore."

"Why does it bother people?"

"Let the dead bury their dead. Times have changed."

"Cousin Fred's house . . ." I looked at the mossy gray house.

"I'd advise you to go home as soon as you can, if you feel this way."

"I want to go home, and yet I want to stay."

"Every time one of the Stevensons died, the Hawaiians would say kahunas were at work. My husband, my daughter, Tony. I want my grandsons to be free of this kind of nonsense. Too many have suffered. Don't bother, Mark! Get a good education and free yourself!"

The things she knew, she would keep to herself. We both fell silent. I thought of Waipio Valley. Fred had said we would go there before the summer was over. I ached to see the falls of Hiilawe, the rich patches of taro, to walk the ground so celebrated in Hawaiian lore.

Mrs. Warrington broke into my reverie. "It's slipped me, Mark, who your mother was. Old age makes one forget."

"She was Agnes Hubbard, from Maui."

"Of course! The Hubbard girls! They lived at Waikapu."

"Those were her aunts. Mumma is an only child."

"I do remember her! A beautiful girl, and very sensitive! She was in San Francisco some years ago. I went there to live after Lemuel died. Your mother was living with an aunt on Pacific Heights. How silly of me to forget *she* married Mark and Ellen's boy—Mark, Junior! Mark, Senior, now! My, he was a rapscallion!"

I laughed. We sat, saying nothing. Mrs. Warrington looked out the window. I fondled the case. I kept thinking about the accident on the slopes of Mauna Kea that had taken Uncle Tony's life.

Mrs. Warrington was talking: "Our ranks are thinning. We seem to be fewer in number with each generation. We are separated now as we never were before. Once there was a whole world of hapa-haoles. Except for our pure Hawaiian relatives, there was no one else. The *others* lived their own lives. At times we'd meet socially—a dinner, a garden fete, a ball at the Palace, one of the Queen's parties. We were happy among ourselves."

"Uncle Beau says it's all different since the days of the monarchy."

"I hesitate to think what will become of Hawaii! A selfish sentiment, don't you think? All of us oldsters hate to see things change. We want life to be as it was when *we* enjoyed it most." She looked at me with her old-court-family lifting of the head and put into my hands a pale-gray sealed envelope on which was my name, swollen with penmanship. "Open it later, dear, when you're alone. I remembered you want to go to Harvard. This other envelope is for the little fellow sitting up there, waiting for you on the wall. I forgot to bring it to the luau on Saturday afternoon."

I was unable to say much. I lowered my head.

After a while Mrs. Warrington said, "That little boy is not well."

I raised my eyes and saw Puna descending the wall and coming toward the car.

"You tell Palani to keep an eye on him! I have a strong feeling he is suffering inwardly! He's practically under a spell!"

I looked at the lightly powdered, slightly rouged, and heavily perfumed dowager. Her face was shaped suddenly into a grimace of evil. "He's *not* under a spell!" I choked, cleared my throat. "But he's very unhappy."

"Hawaiians are funny about children." Her voice was flat, almost without timbre. She broke off. "Sometimes children suffer dreadfully because their elders are poopaakiki. Do you know what I said, Mark?"

"Stubborn."

"More than that—foolishly stubborn! Foolhardy!" She shook her head, closing her eyes. Then she looked brightly at me. "Well, Mark, I must go now, and this is good-bye." She kissed my cheek. Her perfume was the same my aunts used: a scent of Caron's.

The ponderous limousine pulled slowly away

from the stone wall like a great felled tree being dragged off with its roots exposed. I sat for a time on the wall.

"You got someting foah me, Markie?" Puna asked. He reached for the box. I drew it away.

Leihulu came running. "I feenish da puzzle, Markie," she said and then gave her attention to the box in my hands. "*You* lucky buggah, Markie! What she went give you?"

"Just some old thing."

The children followed me to my room, determined to see my gift. I put the box on the breadfruit-design quilt that covered my bed, and laid the gray envelopes next to it as would an acolyte in a communion service.

"Don't be niele," I scolded.

In time I brought out the spurs.

"Wait till Puppa see deze," Leihulu said, her eyes big. She examined carefully the balled end of the goad.

"Gee, Markie! You lucky!" Puna intoned happily, waving the spur he'd picked up.

"These sterling silver spurs belonged to a man who died a long time ago. He was Mrs. Warrington's brother-in-law. His name was Tony."

Leihulu's face gathered into an expression of horror. She threw the spur on the bed. "I no like touch tings dat come from dead people."

She had given the spurs an evil cast. I wanted to shake her. "What about all the furniture and things in this house? This bed, these kapa, these chairs?" I said angrily. "All things come from dead people!"

Her face took on a suspicious, quelled look. "Doze tings are different," she said with a kind of sheepish defiance.

A new feeling welled in me, over which I had no control. I imagined my insides were quivering as I'd seen trees and shrubs do during a protracted earth tremor.

"*Make* man spur! Dead man spur!" Puna chanted, dancing at the edge of my bed, still clutching the one he had picked up.

"No talk like dat, Puna!" Leihulu's eyes seemed to pop. "Put it down!"

"*Make* man spur!" he sang. "Leihulu stay scay-ed of da *make* man spur!" He threw the spur on the floor.

"Both of you get out of my room! I want to write letters. Go on!"

Leihulu took her brother's hand. "Less go. I no like stay heah wit doze *make* man spurs!"

I closed the door and tried to ignore Puna's loud squalling as she pulled him down the hall to the breakfast room. I returned the spurs to their slots in the elegant case. My heartbeat was rapid. It seemed to be growing steadily faster. I walked aimlessly around the room. Sweat formed on my neck, my forehead. I wiped away the moisture with hard, vengeful gestures. My heart pounded so hard I could see my shirt move under the impact of each beat. I tried to lie across the middle of the bed, but the beat of my heart seemed to lift me as though my body were a pneumatic drill bobbing up with each resistance of mortar or stone. I flew out of the room, holding my side. I walked fast to the stable. Henry was there, saddle-soaping bits of tack.

"Wassamatta, Markie?"

I was choking. "Hold my hand, Henalee!"

He dropped the foamy sponge and ran to my side. He gripped one of my hands and with his free hand rubbed my back. My eyes were clouded. Everything seemed to be shimmering. I doubled over. Henry stopped rubbing. "Keep it up!" I yelled. He let go of my hand and rubbed hard along my spine with both fists. I righted myself. He was pounding my back gently. He seemed to know instinctively what to do. Gradually my heart stopped pounding; my breathing and vision went back to normal. I sat on the steps, sweating freely.

"Somebody went hoʻomana you, I teenk!"

"No, I was frightened about something."

"About wat?"

"I don't know," I said irritably.

"You bettah see one doctah!"

"No!"

"Maybe Puppa know wat happen. If you tell heem."

"No. Don't tell anybody! Most of all the kids."

Henry considered this a moment and ambled off. I sat for what seemed a long time and then walked past the place where the goats were tethered to the watercress patch on the stream.

A night heron flew overhead. I was instinctively fearful. They were night birds and brought bad luck to those who saw them by day. I cursed myself for being afraid. Hawaiians see omens in everything. I cursed myself for being Hawaiian. Look at me, I thought, sitting here imagining I'm surrounded by spirits, that they will reveal things to me in the shape clouds take, in the particular rustle of trees when a breeze passes through their foliage, or in the pattern of the water as it passes over rocks. And I was helpless for I could not sort out the good from the evil portents. I thought of Laura, and my skin grew bumpy. I pulled my shirttail out and let my hand run slowly over the goose bumps. It was a pleasant sensation. Still soaked through with fear, I ran eagerly to the Punohu house.

Laura was in the kitchen, stirring something on the wood cookstove. My visit did not seem to surprise her.

"I'm making a custard for my long johns," she said. Near the stove on a counter there was a tray on which a dozen or so of the elongated donuts sat draining cooking oil into the brown paper spread under them.

"Long johns?" I said vacuously.

Laura gave a slight vehemence to her stirring. "You've been having some trouble, Markie."

"Are you a kahuna, Laura?" I asked playfully.

She laughed. "I'd make a fortune if I were, what with all the superstitious people around Waimea."

"What happens, Cousin Laura, when you have one of your spells?"

She laughed again, tinny, high, and thin. "Dead people talk to me," she said in a lifeless voice. "I am a born medium."

Goose bumps formed again all over me. My eyes smarted with tears. I clutched my fist. I wanted to hit something. "Are you a spiritualist?"

She laughed again, this time like an insult. "No, I'm a good Christian." Now she was laughing so hard that she stopped stirring. Her custard nearly boiled over. "My custard!" She dug her spoon into the bubbling yellowish mass, stirred rapidly, carefully, lifted the pot away from the heated iron and gently set it down at the cool end of the stove. "I've spoilt it," she said, as though spitting unwanted pits from her mouth. She dumped the hot custard into the fresh pot. A cloud of steam rose. "Louise will notice. She's very sensitive to tastes." She took the scorched pot to the sink and ran water into it. She sat down near me at the round koa table in the alcove.

"I'm frightened, Cousin Laura. I had a kind of spell about an hour ago."

"What happened, exactly?"

"My heart beat so fast I couldn't count the beats. I felt I was choking. My eyes were blurred."

"Pure panic!" she said flatly. "What exactly is frightening you?"

"I don't know."

"What happened before the attack?"

I told her.

"Why on earth did she give you his spurs?" The smile that had come earlier vanished.

I nervously let my eyes roam. It was hard to explain. My gaze fell to the floor. I studied a pair of ants vainly searching the glossy gray surface for a remnant of food.

"It is strange, but also kind of wonderful." Her eyes lighted up.

"Do you think I should keep them?"

"Of course! They're to be treasured! Sometimes the personal belongings of high-ranking people are filled with mana. Tony's spurs would have good mana." Her expression changed. "Unless someone has smeared them with bad mana since he died. Bring them over to me this evening. Louise would enjoy seeing them too."

Laura would exorcise any vestige of bad mana that clung to them by virtue of her gifts. I knew this, but did not want to acknowledge it consciously.

She rose from the table. "I must fill my long johns before the custard sets."

She looked fragile again—as thin-skinned and colorless as she had been on the night I first met her. I walked to the kitchen door. Before opening it, I wheeled around, decided to speak. "I saw an akualele the night I came over here with Puna!"

Laura jerked.

"It hovered for a while over this house, and then over Uncle Fred's and then it flew away."

Laura seemed to be swooning. Her eyes were shut. Her face was white as porcelain. As she stretched out her arms for support, I helped her to a chair. I was pleased. She could examine my spurs; divest them of bad mana, but she could not have control of me!

"Georgie!" Her voice was like a thin high reed pitched almost above human hearing. "I don't want to be left alone," she murmured, crossing herself in a slow indifferent way, her tiny fingers like pale tapers as she drew them across her flat breast.

As I stumbled blindly from the Ponohu house, I had a sickening sense that Leihulu—and then Laura in her trance—had made it impossible for me to enjoy ownership of something that I should treasure. Even Puna's smile and childlike remarks could not change my mood. I needed to be alone. I felt weary. Puna seemed to cling to me like a spider web. I could pack my bags and have Joe drive me to Kawaihae where I could wait for the little cattle ship; but Joe was still in Kona. I lighted the kerosene lamp. Black smoke billowed up in streaks from the small opening at the top of the chimney. Again my thoughts churned within my mind. What signs are in the smoke? Is there a sign in the smell of the oil? I blew out the flame. The room smelled of mold. Would I spend the rest of my life being pushed by the need to interpret *signs* as they appeared? Is this the way Hawaiians live? I sat in one of the rocking chairs, willing myself to be as inert, as feelingless as the wood of the chair. Was it, too, filled with mana? Bad or good? Had Uncle Palani or Great-aunt Louise imbued the chair with the unpleasantness of their quarrels? Or was it a harbinger of their strength? The four-poster? More pain, more grief?

I remembered that I'd tucked Mrs. Warrington's envelope under the quilt. I leaped from the chair and unsealed the envelope, careful not to rip it unnecessarily. There was a note and a gray-green check written against funds in the Morgan Guaranty and Trust Company, Paris, France, for a thousand dollars. I was impressed by the masculinity of the signature: A. D. Warrington. Dizzy, I leaned on the bed and read: "Dear Mark—You said you wanted to go to Harvard. Here is something to help you get there. Put it away now in a special account until the time comes for you to go. Think of it as a gift from Uncle Tony Stevenson and Eben, along with the spurs. With my best wishes and aloha—" It was signed: "Aunt Nita."

The silver spurs regained their original significance: a source of strength and joy. Eben had actually given up his ownership in order that I might have them. Anything belonging to him could not be steeped in bad mana. I would gladly show the spurs to Laura and Louise. I felt they were now really beyond Laura's reach. I was linked now to Eben as I had been since childhood to Uncle Tony Stevenson. Years later it came to me that the connection was an aesthetic one.

I walked purposelessly from one end of the room to the other. Finally I shed my boots and jacket and stretched out across the middle of the bed. When I awoke it was raining. Puna was asleep near me at the foot of the bed, his arm crooked around the box of spurs, the kapa serving as his pillow. I found the envelopes on the floor, blown there by the sudden wind that had brought the rain upon us.

In Waimea, a wind blows up with uncanny abruptness, followed by mists or fog. The skies turn a wet gray, the air cools, moistens, and torrential rain falls. Waimea weather has the power and violence of the volcanic peaks, the luxuriance of the wet upland forests: an atmosphere too rich, too dramatic for the human scale. At such times, one needed to do small stupid things. I herded the children into the kitchen to cook a huge pot of chopped cabbage and kaluaed pork and two dozen oversized muffins.

Fred rode in furiously, early in the afternoon, draped in a great wet oilskin. He dismounted at the pomelo tree and called out for Joe. From the kitchen porch I yelled that Joe had not come home yet. Fred's high squeals were probably oaths. The rain came at the earth in white sheets, beating on the corrugated tin roof of the kitchen wing.

I enjoyed Fred's sour reaction to my being given the spurs. He had been so censorious of my referring to "Uncle Tony."

"Just like those rich people to do such damn-fool things. Those fancy ball-end spurs ain't worth a damn when you really need to work up a horse."

I did not mention my check. Fred was preoccupied with Puna's for one hundred dollars, drawn on a local bank.

The next day was bright and sunny. Lepeka began bringing her personal belongings. She entered into the act of becoming the new mistress of the much-widowed household with the solemnity of someone taking religious vows. Her laughter was less free; her green eyes, less playful. She put her oblong cases, filled with the accumulation of her years of maidenhood, in the master bedroom of Uncle Palani's suite, saying, "I think Analu an' me stay in diss room aftah we ma'lee."

Fred was not so committal when he saw the room that evening. "Damn women! They can accumulate more junk."

"Aunty come stay wit us?" Puna asked me from time to time as Lepeka came and went that day, driven by an uncle who owned a Model T Ford.

"Hasn't Puppa told you he's going to marry Aunty Lepeka?"

A pleading look accompanied the denial.

"Yes, Puna, she's going to be your new mother. She's coming here to live." I sounded like an English governess.

Puna went to my room, crawled into a corner and bawled for most of an hour. Henry threatened to ship him. I took him for a walk, and his spirits brightened.

Leihulu willingly helped Lepeka unpack the woven cases. Lepeka proudly brought out items to show the girl, who responded with suitable gushings. They chattered like schoolgirls, growing more intimate after each feast of giggles and talk. Leihulu instinctively seized Lepeka as a cohort after months of being the solitary girl in a household of males and a farm full of animals.

In the early part of the morning Henry had gone his own way, searching for chicken or guinea fowl eggs, checking the goats and pigs. Faithfully and with little effort, it seemed, he fed the pups and kittens and saw to it that there was corn scattered in a bare spot in the kitchen garden for the chickens and ducks.

Joe arrived late in the morning with a number of bundles, *pu-olu,* loaded on him by his ohana at Kona. The sampan jitney deposited him squarely in front of the house, across the highway. He made two trips, Henry helping, across the road, carrying packages and placing them first on top of the stile.

The bounty from Joe's cousins was added to the delectables still remaining from the luau, and we feasted in the kitchen sans the company of the two womenfolk who were again at the Launuis' collecting Lepeka's belongings. After lunch, Joe proceeded with the arduous duty of slaughtering the remaining wild goat. Conscientiously, Henry assisted him.

Later in the day, I heard Lepeka ask Joe about Julian. When she was out of sight and hearing, he said to me, "Why she cay-ah weah Julian stay? Not her business!"

"You so smaht, Sonny," she said to me, "how to cook haole kau-kau! I like verrrry much! Ono loa ka mea ai haole! Anty onny know how foa-ah cook pipi stew, palai an' na mea ai Hawaii."

"I'll teach . . ."

Her answer was a smile as wide as the Pacific Ocean. She was so bold-faced in hinting that, even after she became mistress of the household, I should continue being the family cook. There was great charm in her cheek.

As I cooked a meat loaf, she asked me about the whip fight. Had Julian been badly hurt? She seemed to gloat over certain details, encouraging me to add gory embellishments.

Fred announced abruptly that he was riding early in the morning to Mahike and would spend the night at the ditchman Moriyama's house. He ordered me to go with him.

"I'll get Lepeka to come and stay with the kids," he said.

"Moriyama built himself a Japanese-style house and surrounded it with a Japanese garden among those big koa and ohi'a trees. You never saw such stands of ekaha growing wild. You know what those are?" Fred asked me, as before daybreak, we headed for the great Kohala Mountains.

"Bird's nest fern."

"Thousands of 'em growing on rocks, in the crotches of trees. Some spread twenty feet across. Old as Methuselah! You can't imagine the varieties of ferns! We'll get some. Pack 'em up in moss for you to take home to Mother. She loves potted plants."

Trees still dripped moisture from a heavy shower in the night. Squeaks and slurpy sounds broke the early morning stillness as our horses' hooves sank into the soggy earth and pulled out. The spirited horses and the rain-charged landscape tapped my store of resilience.

We passed a large old house amidst unkempt lawns.

"The Merton house, Markie," Fred slowed his horse for a moment. "Now if I was your age I'd have found my way here a long time ago. Have you seen those beautiful girls?"

"They are good riders. Fine horses."

"Old Kualoha Merton was some dish in her day!"

We passed a cluster of shops and a gas station: Omura Store, Kanasaki Shoten, Lau Tang's Store.

"Lau Tang's the local bootlegger. These Chinamen have gotten rich selling booze!" Fred's eyes gleamed.

"It's against the law."

"Live and let live!" He was grinning, his face as pink as the inside of a seashell.

We rode past Judge Peyton's sprawling white house, sitting in a grove of Monterey cypress. A deep horseshoe drive led under a low porte cochere.

"That's where the knot's to be tied. This will be his fourth fee from me, by golly!"

Towering trees swayed wildly as the morning wind howled through their branches. The first pink signs of dawn appeared above the northeastern slopes of Mauna Kea.

"You were right, Markie. Puna is behaving in a peculiar way."

My surprise moved me to say: "He's one of the nicest little fellows I've ever known."

"You make me very happy, Markie." Fred's voice was gentle. "My God, but his mother was a jewel. As beautiful within as she was on the outside. Never said a cross word."

"I hear that . . . Puna looks like her and Julian, too, if you don't mind my saying so."

"He was her brother, but Miriam had none of his filthy-mindedness. I hope that evil creature never lays a hand on my boy again. If he ever shows up, Mark, for any reason at all, you tell him to get going! If he doesn't heed, you go for Moki, the policeman! I mean this, Mark!"

Ernest Moluhi and Kapua Gomes were joining us to make another attempt to bring in the renegade longhorn bulls that were hampering the ranch program to produce a pure strain of Herefords. Moluhi worried me; he seemed so lacking in Polynesian friendliness. He greeted me with an indifferent grunt, and began immediately to converse, amiably enough, with Fred.

On our right were *kuleanas* of homesteaders and crop farmers: long narrow strips of acreage on flat land. Beyond them Mauna Kea loomed, reaching up, as was said in one of the chants, "To grasp the eyeball of Heaven." In the foot hills were scattered kuleanas bounded by log fences like pioneer homesteads, with a few head of cattle and small flocks of sheep, chickens, and occasional flocks of turkey and coveys of guinea fowl. Even the CCC camp with its collection of long, low-lying barracks-type buildings, painted dark green—which had a kind of industrial look about them—failed to affect the general appearance of Waimea as a rural Hawaiian community. As we rode, Fred gave me a running inventory. The homesteaders kept dairy herds or a few steers or raised pigs. The crop farmers, mostly Japanese, grew flowers for the Honolulu markets and first-rate, cool-weather vegetables, such as iceberg lettuce, celery, or broccoli.

We turned into a dirt road lined with towering gum trees that led deceptively into the wilderness of finely grassed paddocks and the dark moist forest of koa and lehua trees. At the end of the eucalyptus-shaded way, we saw Kapua Gomes mounted on a massive, spirited blue roan mare. Duke snorted pettishly as we approached. In the dawn light, Kapua's eyes bore their same love-hungry message.

"Today you going see some ack-shun, boy! Going make da time we wen' foah da wile peegs look like one birt'day pah-ty!"

We first encountered the longhorns in a grassy ravine. A heavy mist hovered like smoke over a ranch herd of cows, two bulls, and scores of half-grown calves in the instinctual protective circle, the cows moving continuously; the great bulls bellowing deeply.

Gomes and Fred cut out one of the bulls. It was bleeding and limped badly.

"Wild bull's been here scrapping with that fella," said Fred. "That's what's worried this herd. The wild buggah must have run off when he heard or smelled us coming. Bastards can hear as well as bats!"

We galloped off after Gomes. It was the first time I'd seen my cousin work the lordly Duke into a fast run. Moluhi followed close behind on his red roan, Laughing Boy. I brought up the rear, clutching my hat, not wanting to have to retrieve it. My old Black Beauty, once he fell into the spirit of the chase, steadily gained on the two younger horses. I saw the shouting men hard after two wild longhorns, heading for a spot deeply wooded with ohi'a. The cattle crashed into the gray-green wall of lehua trees. Fred veered Duke skillfully from the path of a huge log, spat and cursed.

We collected at the edge of the forest. It was no longer misty, but the skies were still overcast with gray. The hard gallop had winded me. In the trees, rocks, and logs, the great ferns unfurled their stiff wide ribbons like tentacles of giant octopi turned upside down.

"Bring a gun nex' time," Gomes said.

"Baxter thinks they should be brought in and slaughtered. Can't blame him, he's gotta think of profits."

We passed through regions thickly grown with towering, ancient tree fern and into wet, foggy ravines. We heard longhorns moving swiftly and stealthily through the brooding woods, quiet, except when one of their great hooves broke off a dry branch or snapped a stick in the path of their escape from the sight or smell of us.

In the late afternoon, we emerged from a ravine

thick with fern and koa onto a little well-cleared knoll. The diminutive house of Saturo Moriyama was a plain, oblong, wood construction, embellished with Japanese touches: peaked roof, curving points where the roof joints met, and shoji doors.

"Ho! Moriyama-san!" Fred shouted from outside the stone wall that surrounded the garden.

"Haddo, Andrew-san!" Moriyama in starched, blue denim trousers and jacket appeared at the bamboo gate.

"Hai, hai, Moriyama-san!"

"Mai, mai, come, come," the little man said in a husky voice. "I make hoch watta—suppose you dike take baht!"

The smell of burning wood and charcoal mingled with odors from the surrounding woodland into a pungent sweetness.

"Goddamn but the air is good up here!" Fred declared, taking in deep breaths as he stood surveying the little homesite. An arched cement bridge led over a clear water brooklet that wound its way from the side of the house to collect in a pool at the front, inhabited by fat slow-moving carp, colored brilliant orange, white, and black, with here and there a mottled stray. Clipped shrubs were planted in groupings of rock, some natural, others arranged—a microcosm of the surrounding landscape. Over the house entrance grew a juniper set leaning by the prevailing wind, its main trunk and larger branches covered with mosses and lichens, a patina of springy textures and muted colors.

"You wanta see me boil in that hot water riggin' of yours, I know!" Fred blustered. "Goddamned tree! I'll be damned if it don't look like somebody chewed the hell outa one side of it!" Fred crouched on a stool at the stoop and laboriously unbooted himself.

I elected to stay outdoors in the soft air to watch the night fall on Moriyama's unexpected domain. The cool moistness and humus-rich soil of the region had made it possible for Moriyama to create an illusion of the home he left when little older than I.

Moluhi joined me. "I no like dis place," he shuddered.

"I do," I said emphatically, wanting to shake him off.

"Das cause you one haole. Way-ah you going sleep tonight, boy?"

"On the floor, I suppose. Isn't that where Japanese people sleep?"

"I sleep nex to you. Tomorrow I go out, try get da pipi laho huihui! I gotta have gooood sleep tonight."

We had brought one of Great-aunt Louise's kapas for Moriyama's young bride, Kimiko, and homemade sausage, a smoked turkey, two pheasants, and strips of salted pork, contributed by Lepeka from the Launui house. The huge repast was served daintily on a low round table at which we sat with our legs crossed. Fred grew more grandiosely gay and high-spirited as the evening progressed, playing drunken but restrained court to Kimiko who moved about deftly and continuously to serve us from a burning brazier and a rice pot.

"Very efficient and wifely!" Fred pronounced. "Very humble, as all women should be. You can't beat these picture brides!"

He was getting something quite different in Lepeka Lovelace.

Kapua Gomes and the silent fear-stricken Moluhi ate and drank with enormous dedication. Between mouthfuls, Kapua showered the elaborately modest hostess with appreciative growls.

Talk recalled the epic round-ups of the past. Fred could boast of participating in those prior to Albert Baxter's modernization of the ranch. Gomes and Moluhi could only bask in their dead fathers' exploits. Gomes' father had told him several thousand wild turkey had once been gathered in the great koa trees on Mauna Kea and sent to markets in Honolulu, where people had complained the flesh tasted of the fern shoots on which the turkeys fed. Fred told of famous old bulls that were tracked down and shot after years of freedom and hell-raising among the new herds of pure-bred Herefords. "They would have made the ones we saw today look like heifers!" he boasted.

Moluhi told of ghostly happenings in his birthplace, Waipio Valley: dogs and cats growing to enormous size on the lonely dark trails. Only if you could resist the night-hypnotism of the spirits, could you shout obscenities at them or urinate to make them disappear. Gomes told of hearing ghostly processions pass his cottage on dark nights of the moon and how his grandmother had advised him to lie flat on the floor and be very still. Fred declared it all crazy nonsense and asked Moriyama to sing.

"You singo firs', boss!"

"Hell, man! I've got the worst voice in the whole of Waimea!" he shrieked and fell into a wild fit of coughing.

Fred had grown alarmingly florid, his skin as taut and red as a radish. I handed him his concertina.

"Never let it be known that Fred Andrews ever refused to be accommodating! I should come by singing naturally. Both my parents had beautiful singing voices!"

"Singo, Andrew-san! Singo!"

Moluhi glared at Fred with red eyes, muttering portentous Hawaiian curses on Fred's disdain of his spirits. Reluctantly he went to get his guitar. Kapua Gomes unearthed an ukulele. Moriyama swayed with the rhythms. Kimiko cleared the table and disappeared from view.

"Now it's your turn, Moriyama!"

"Kimiko-san!" Moriyama called several times, but there was no answer.

I went to the little kitchen and then outside to the connecting woodshed. I heard sobbing, soft, graceful, like the cry of certain birds who loiter and feed along marshy beaches. She was embarrassed when she saw me. I pointed to the house, and she sped to her husband's side. I heard rousing applause.

Kimiko began to pluck her samisen slowly, giving Moriyama the chance to gather himself. He sang playfully but with restraint. He was not a professional, he explained, in a flood of sucked-in and spat-out phrases.

The words and manifests of emphasis and restraint in the half-spoken, recitative song prompted me to whisper to Fred, "This is like old Japan, like the screens at the Academy of Arts."

"Bull shit!" he squealed, rolling his china-blue eyes. "This is Puukapu."

"Nudda song! Nudda song!" Gomes sounded like one of the bulls of the disturbed herd.

"Hana hou! Hana hou!" Moluhi grunted in echo.

Kimiko's head was bowed, and in Japanese Moriyama gave her instructions with a gruffness I'd not seen before. During the long years of his bachelorhood, Moriyama had come to depend on such sporadic debauches. This was the first since Kimiko had joined him.

Quite suddenly Fred fell from a sitting position into a deep, snoring sleep. With a noisome struggle, we put him to bed in the little room the ditchman indicated, where Kimiko hurriedly arranged sleeping pads and splashy patterned quilts. Gomes began with inebriate dolefulness to sing a fado. A note of desire had crept into his voice.

Moriyama went to his room and passed out. Moluhi found a corner of the main room, safe from his dreaded Hawaiian ghosts. Gomes' singing had come to a tearful conclusion.

Outside, the night was very dark, the stars very

brilliant. I could hear the smallest sounds that insects make. The air, clear of fog, moved me to inhale deeply till I trembled.

I heard Kimiko's faint cries coming from the kitchen side of the garden. I crossed the arched bridge. Kapua Gomes held her tightly around the waist and was trying to kiss her. I went to him, and he knocked me over with a quick blow of his arm.

"You bugga, I going geev you good leeking!"

"You can't do this!" I said from the ground.

"No can do!" Kimiko chanted with some Japanese words and freed herself with a single concentrated push. She ran into the house with the tiniest steps imaginable.

"You'll get in trouble!" I said, gasping and rising.

In a moment his great, tautly-muscled arms encircled my body. "You one Goddamn good keed! You save Kapua from planny trouble!" He lifted me from the ground and twirled unsteadily, pressing his sandpaper-bearded face against mine.

"Go to sleep," I said, squirming free. "You have plenty to do in the morning!"

"Right now I gotta take a leek!" he said in a deep guttural and fell in a heap on the ground.

It was one of the physical triumphs of my life to get him settled into his sleeping place in the main room. I spread a thick cotton-battened quilt over the paniolos and walked off, muttering obscenities.

I fell on my sleeping pad in Fred's room, now reeking of his liquor. His wretched snoring drove me to sleep.

It was three in the morning when I awoke, hearing faint, childlike sobs again, through the collective snoring of the four men. It was cold. The crying stopped. I thought of the clear heavens, the dark trees, roaming pigs, and Moluhi's and Gomes' ghosts. From curiosity or portent, I threw off the quilt and rose.

A dim light led me to three steps and a little room. A small lantern rested on a low table, its flickering light lingering on the gilded metal fittings of a small cabinet. Before it, in a precisely achieved position, Kimiko Moriyama sat.

I went to her. In a whisper I asked if something was wrong. With a gesture soft as a falling feather, she motioned for me to sit on her quilts. I assumed her position, as best I could. We sat this way a long time.

She began to fondle my hair. She ran her fingers over my cheeks and neck. She unbuttoned my shirt, wheeled round, and, still sitting, reached for something under a shelf. She turned back, holding masks. She put one over my face and covered hers with the other. I accepted mine with misgivings, but they were not those about what mana or signs it contained. She wheeled round again, lifted her mask, and blew out the lantern.

We left the ditchman's house at daybreak, the three men red-eyed, numbed, unspeaking. I was feeling successive waves of gloating, embarrassment and shame. Moriyama sleepily bade us good-bye after serving us bowls of hot tea, hardtack and jam. Kimiko did not appear.

We rode for a long time in silence on trails overhung with maile vine. The air was cool and clean, and the skies open. I wondered what Kapua's reaction would be if I told him what had happened. My previous knowledge of sex came from obscure, most often humorous allusions and metaphors in Hawaiian songs and conversations. I could not make them jibe with my experience in the night.

We came on a wild bull and cow feeding at the edge of a shallow gully, strategically close to the ohi'a woods. Fred said they were the same pair we'd run into the morning before. We rode within fifty yards of the beasts before they sprinted. Fred raced Duke along the edge of the woods and headed the cattle off. The paniolos followed, waiting for Fred's signal. When he gave it, Moluhi threw his lariat first and caught the cow around her horns. Gomes and Fred both missed the bull just as it crashed into a thicket of tree fern.

"Goddamit-to-hell!" Fred shrieked, wheeled round, and raced back with Gomes to Moluhi to help with the cow.

"We'll use the bitch for bait! That old bugga's been screwin' the hell outa her!" Fred pulled hard on his reins. Duke made beautiful prancing movements. "He'll come back for his sweetheart, don't worry!"

The cowboys secured the cow to an ohi'a stump, away from the protective trees and giant ferns. Kimiko invaded my thoughts continually with euphoria. I fenced off shame with complacency and felt at peace. Waimea seemed unthreatening and wonderful.

We rode two hundred yards upwind to a ravine filled with bird's nest fern.

"We'll gather up some ferns for the boy here to take home. We can take turns checking from the hapu'upu'u," he gestured to a nearby knoll, his eyes twinkling, "to see if old Valentino has shown up to claim his one and only."

I laughed often as we took the carefully selected ferns from their lifetime perches on rocks and tree trunks, secured their fronds with strands of maile vine, and bundled them on the pack horses. The ferns exuded their peculiar fragrance; the maile vines, their spicy perfume. Fred, by seniority and inclination, took the first watch for the bull.

Gomes and Moluhi selected luxuriant tips of maile vine, stripped them from the stem, and piled the pliant strands for weaving into leis. I contributed by separating the fragrant leafy garlands and laying each strip to lie free of another.

"Diss keed ees really eleu," Gomes said to Moluhi.

We laughed, joyous, as though preparing the rites of the hula goddess Laka. There was almost a feminine gentleness in the way the paniolos pursued the making of the maile leis. They would change if the wild bull joined its cow. Gomes wound a particularly handsome strand around my hat and placed a handful of longer strips over my shoulders.

"Eef you was one wahine, Markie, I geev you one keez now!"

"Kiss me anyhow," I said with bravado and turned my cheek.

Moluhi chuckled and muttered something in Hawaiian.

"Wat da hell, why not!" Gomes said and planted a hairy kiss on my cheek. "You taught I no was going take you up on dat, eh, Markie?"

"I knew you would."

"Kolohe no keia keiki hapa-haole hanohano," was Moluhi's comment, offered with a smile of uncharacteristic gentleness, but I did not like being called a mischievous young half-white of the gentry.

"Keiki hapa-haole he mea lapu-wale!" Gomes added with an explosive laugh. His Hawaiian use of a negative remark to express affection had Moluhi chuckling.

"So you think I'm a worthless hapa-haole," I said. "What about you, you hapa-pokiki?"

He laughed again loudly. "Yeah, I'm one wort'less half-portagee."

We fell silent as Fred rode up. "He'll be there before long. Just try and keep him away. . ."

"From his lady love!" I interjected.

Fred gave me a sharp look. "Maile leis? Ain't you guys got something better to do than this?" He banded his hat with a wad of the entwined strings of leaves.

The men roped the great bull that day, and slaughtered it on the spot. I walked away.

"Ain't you goina give us a hand, boy?" Fred said with a commanding gesture.

"Leave um go, Fred! The boy's not used to these Waimea celebrations," Gomes said. He used the expression *ka hookaulana ana* for celebration, one I had not often heard.

Moluhi claimed the fat liver, perfect for eating raw, Hawaiian-style.

We rode, carrying the gory sections to the main road, men and horses decked with copious garlands of maile. I was depressed at leaving the wilderness of Mahike. The memory of the night surged up. The smell of the maile and fern mixed with the distinct odor of raw beef suddenly had me almost retching. I was uncomfortable riding because the ferns had been transferred to Black Beauty to leave room on the other horses for the meat. I became morbidly concerned about possible damage to the ferns.

In the tree-shaded avenue, Gomes asked me when I was going home.

"Next week, I think."

Fred grimaced and cleared his throat.

"I take you up Mauna Kea. We go Keeaumoku spen' da night. You see da wile turkeys an' da Hawaiian birds."

"Pretty dangerous traveling in that country! That plant man David Douglas lost his life up there. Fell into a volcanic pit." Fred was unsmiling, high-voiced, business-like.

"I know my way aroun' dat country, Analu," Gomes said.

"Pretty chancy," Fred persisted. "Area is swarming with wild bulls. There are native birds still there. If there are any o-o left, they are at Keeaumoku."

We rode on in silence.

Black Beauty became worrisome once we left the shaded road and entered the highway. He began at first to trot slowly. When I made no effort to rein in, he increased his speed. Fred called out. The horse worked to a canter. Fred called out more sharply. I was now a hundred or so yards ahead of him and the paniolos. The panic was on me again. My hands and feet were tingling. I dug my heels into the horse's flanks. He charged. The ferns, fixed to my cantles, flapped loudly as we passed groups of children playing in front of homesteaders' cottages. I could hear the snapping of Fred's bullwhip. Anger added to my panic. I urged the black horse into a full gallop. Trees, houses, and people streaked by. I lost control, except to keep my hands on the reins and my feet pressed on the stirrups. What I was doing was against the most sacred local rules of horsemanship. It was indulgent, wanton! Ka uha'uha a me ka lapuwale! We raced on, both horse and boy under a spell. I felt a wicked, utterly debauching exhilaration on top of my panic. I felt totally mad!

The front gate was open. I had imagined, as we flew past the Punohu house, that my horse, for all his fourteen years, would leap it before I had a chance to pull him in from the five-mile run.

Joe ran out from the kitchen, followed by Lepeka and Henry. "Wassamatta, Markie?" he yelled as I passed him, running toward the house.

"He's frightened, perhaps? See how white he is!" Lepeka said, coming toward me. I struggled to understand her Hawaiian.

I tore into my room, pulled my two suitcases from under the bed, and began packing. My hands and body were shaking. I was crying. Lepeka came in, followed by Henry.

"Heaha ia oe?"

"Nothing!" I answered angrily.

"Please, Sonny, tell Aunty! We have trouble oursel' today. We no can fine Puna! Au'we ka pilikia nui loa la!"

"*Namu haole!* Speak English!" I growled.

"C'mon, Markie, no talk to Aunty like dat!" Henry scolded.

"You know I no speak haole good." Lepeka's voice was quavery.

The sharp reports of Fred's whip sounded over the house. "Where is that horse killer?"

Lepeka ran to Uncle Palani's porch. "Aale huhu,

Analu! We have enough trouble as it is!"

"All the way home! He rode my Black Beauty at full gallop!" he shrieked and cracked the whip.

Leihulu came sleepily into my room, crying and inquiring. I raced out through the porch, past Lepeka, to the pomelo tree, where I stood, my arms drawn tight against my sides.

Fred wheeled Duke around. The great horse reared. Fred cracked the whip again. Lepeka flew past me to the side of the horse. There was liquor on her breath. Somewhere in the swirls of her appeals, she was able to say that Puna was missing. He responded with a long wail, got off his horse, and began to abuse Lepeka for drinking.

"What in God's name have I done to deserve all this?" Fred moaned. "Have you called Moki? Have you gotten anyone to help?"

Lepeka broke down. Leihulu put her arms around her and joined in the bawling.

I went to my room and sat in one of the rockers. All I could think was to get to Kawaihae and wait for a ship. There would be one leaving in the morning or the day after. The ferns were ruined. I was sure the horse would live. Fred had been humiliated that someone in his family had galloped a horse down the side of the highway. I felt calmer, but, surely, it was time for me to leave. I did not hear Puna enter my room in the darkness.

"I was ovah da kine—da stable."

"Across the street? Puppa is worried!"

The child began to cry.

"It's all right, Puna. You're safe. That's the important thing."

He came with me to the kitchen. Fred lunged for him. I pulled Puna back. Fred pushed me aside and grabbed the boy. Lepeka protested, whimpering, her face flushed a bright coppery red. Fred held the child's head between his crooked left arm and walloped his backside with the other. "I told you never to leave this place!"

Puna screamed.

"Please, Uncle Fred, that's enough! Please!" I stood before him.

Lepeka sashayed in one direction, then another, pleading in Hawaiian. Fred stopped spanking and released Puna, who ran toward me, hollering my name. I took him and began to leave the room.

"Markie! I'm not through with you!"

I stopped, wheeled around, and said: "I'm truly sorry, Uncle Fred, I ran Black Beauty home. I lost my head."

"Lawa, Analu! Lawa!" Lepeka pleaded.

"More Goddamned nonsense going on around here than you can shake a stick at! I don't know what I've done to deserve all this!" He reached for his prized decanter and poured a walloping drink.

Puna's sobbing continued until he fell asleep an hour or so later. Fred and Lepeka retired to the parlor with the decanter and a pitcher of water. Some of their conversation seeped into the breakfast room. Lepeka suggested that Fred send for a kahuna in Kohala: an ancient woman renowned for her powers who could "smell out" the person responsible for the hoo hewa being brought on Puna.

Joe shook his head. "*Now* we have trouble. *Now* we see some ack-shun! Auwe! *When* Hawaiian peoples going learn to leave diss pilau stuff alone?"

We all shivered.

"She gifted," Lepeka continued. "She from da ol' school. She help us."

Fred reprimanded her for speaking so loudly. He popped back into the breakfast room where we sat and ordered Henry and Leihulu to skiddadle.

From my room, sitting quiet as owls at noon, we heard the discussion continue in the breakfast room. Fred insisted he would use someone *he* knew to "help out"—an old man who lived in Waipio. Lepeka was familiar with the old man's name. She agreed he was oihana hemolele, gifted in dispelling evil spirits, but she clung to the idea that the woman *she* recommended was the best kahuna kuni ola on the island, who could divine in one session the source of the trouble that had fallen on Fred's house.

Fred sent Joe after Ben, who would be more successful on the Waipio mission. Ben was patient with these people, ke la poʻe. Ben knew how to pray with them, to sit for hours listening to the repetitive incantations of these "gifted ones." He could take one of the pigs to the old man at Waipio, some of the smoked fowl and meat, and money. "My son is a college graduate, but he respects the old ways. He will help us." Lepeka urged Fred to go to Waipio himself. "Or send for the wise one to come here! He can kalana pule, say the needed prayers, on the spot!" she argued. From my bedroom window, we saw Joe drive off in the old Packard.

"Ain't notting wrong wit Puna! He jes' acking funny," Henry said.

"I scay-ed!" Leihulu sat close to Henry.

"Puna is lonesome" I said, trying to hold back tears. "Aren't there any kids he could play with around here?"

"Puppa no like us play wit nobody. He say we gotta mine our own business an' let dem mine dere's."

Fred had made a rule for himself and family—to live in detachment from other people. We were prisoners of our family fortune's decline.

Someone was walking in the little hall above my room.

"Puppa's going to pray to his Goddamn stones!" said Henry.

I wanted to take one of the pieces of firewood, go upstairs and club Fred.

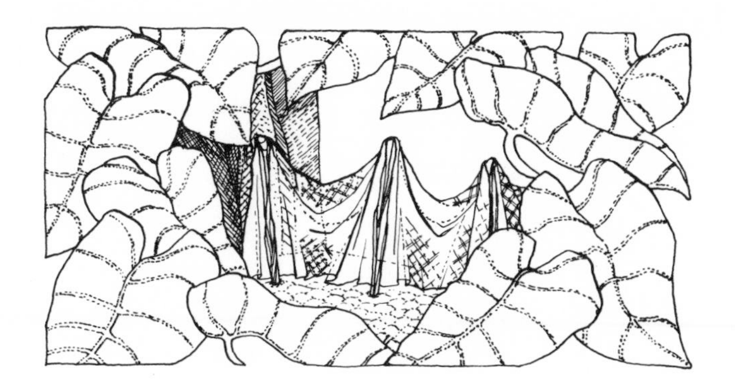

In the morning, Ben Andrews and I started for Waipio in his Ford.

"I have one or two stops to make, and it takes time to ride down the cliff side into the valley. Puppa has sent word for them to have donkeys waiting for us at the Lookout," he explained.

I hoped he'd have something to say about the real purpose of the visit.

"Once in a while, I go and check on Dad's land down there to see how the taro crop is coming along, or to check up on people who haven't paid their rent."

Descriptions of Ben had not prepared me for his imperial bearing, the rock-like solidity of his head and the stillness with which it sat, with its mass of dark curly hair, upon his neck, which was as thick as the trunk of a half-grown lehua tree and as smoothly round. His yellowish-gray eyes had the same air of quietude, of hauteur as unaffected as a great stone.

He drove his car with a lackadaisical indifference to time. We crept past a well-fenced place with excellent stands of grazing. A little house sat in a clump of Monterey cypress at the top of a gently rising hillock about a half-mile from the road. Cattle and a few fat horses fed in the waist-high grass.

"My place," Ben said. "My mother left it to my brothers and me. I lease from them."

"You're a rancher?"

"A real small one. I like to breed horses. It's in our blood. My grandfather . . ."

"They say Uncle Palani had the best horses round here in his day."

"I've read his log books. He knew what he was doing."

"I'd like to see them!"

"Have you enjoyed your visit here? Is the place what you thought it might be?"

"It's certainly different from Honolulu."

We were descending the northern slope of Mauna Kea. The sea was in sight, a blue waste dotted with white spots, ridiculously enormous. When we came to the Honoka'a Junction to make the left turn to the Waipio Valley Lookout, Ben pulled to the side of the road, pondered a moment, and then said solemnly: "I'd like to take something for the folks at Waipio."

We turned right and drove for a block or so to Miyashiro's General Store. I was ready to stretch my legs, tired from the meandering pace and languid conversation.

Ben searched the shelves for canned Alaska sockeye slamon, selected a side of salted salmon from a barrel, and picked up a five gallon can of Saloon Pilot crackers. He bought several pounds of various Chinese preserved fruits: li hing mui, si mui, hum lum, mango seed, and the sticky soursweet salty "crack seed," which Mr. Miyashiro laboriously shovelled out of a large glass jar.

"The kids like this rubbish."

"How about salted duck eggs?"

"They put down their own. I'll go for some beer, Markie, while you take this stuff to the car."

He sauntered out.

"Hi! Ya! Too much biggo man, Ben Androo, noh?" Mr. Miyashiro's mouth exploded when he talked.

"Yeah, him numbah one biggo," I replied.

We drove on silently toward Kukuihaele.

"My father neglects Puna," Ben said finally. "Little fella looks awful!"

He eased the car onto the shoulder as a pickup truck approached. Two half-grown boar carcasses, their tusks beginning to curve, were set atop the front fenders, their massive heads looking like baroque gargoyle headlights. A pack of blood-and-mud-smeared dogs wavered in the bed of the truck. The Stetson-shaped lauhala hats of the three men in the front seat were wound with fresh maile vines. After exchanging greetings and news with Ben, they roared off in low gear, the spicy smell of their leis, gas and oil fumes, dogs, pigs, and human sweat odors trailing behind.

Ben drove on at the same slow pace. White and yellow ginger, at the height of the blooming season, grew in large, luxuriant clusters along the roadside wherever there was water from irrigation ditches or seepage from the foothills. The fragrance was quite different from the heavier, more penetrating redolence of the magnolias and pak lan at Waimea.

"How do you size up what's happened to Puna?" Ben spoke heavily now.

"I think he's lonely. Maybe he needs kids his own age." I studied Ben's face with its Andrews gravity: a Waimea expression. "Puna misses Julian."

"Julian's deep in some ways and just a kid in others. He should have had more schooling."

"Why does your father accuse Julian of being a kahuna?"

Ben gave me the sharp look I expected. "It's serious business. Ghosts are a lot of bull shit, but kahunas are real people. I've seen their work. It's enough to make you piss in your pants!"

"Your father thinks Puna is being kahunaed."

"I don't think it's possible to pray a child to death. I'm going to Waipio just to appease Dad." His gaze roamed down to the sea a thousand feet below us. "I have to keep my thoughts straight."

"Julian is really attached to Puna."

"Too attached, if you ask me! Hawaiian love. They believe in having peoples' souls! Julian is from the old school. I think he knows a hell of a lot, but I *don't* think he's a kahuna! It takes more training than he could possibly have had at Waimea without Dad knowing about it."

It was late in the day when we made our descent of the valley wall, taking a narrow rocky path on the donkeys that had been sent up for us.

"Heha Waipio i ka noe. You know what that means?" Ben asked. "Waipio is drowsing in the mist. You find it in the songs. You hear it when the old-timers speak. Wait till you see this place. Wait till you meet the people. It's still God's country down here. No one rushes. No one frets. Everybody's doors are open and there's plenty to eat. And love, my boy! Love!" Ben was beaming. "It's yours for the asking down here. You know what I mean?"

"I guess so," I said, clutching my donkey's cropped mane.

I was turned over to Abraham Hanohano, the patriarch of the renowned part-Hawaiian Johnson family, which put us up. The family had owned the fishing rights of Waipio for generations. Ben left to distribute his largesse.

"Would you like to see our establishment?" the old man asked me in English. His accent was disarmingly cultivated. He was dressed in clean khaki trousers lopped off below the knee with unhemmed frayed edges. He wore no belt, and the top button was left free over his remarkably unprotruding middle. The bare torso was hairless and showed only slight signs of age. "There are several buildings. We are a large family."

A large frame house was connected by elevated boardwalks to the wooden buildings around it. One of these was a big shed without walls in which nets, hundreds of feet long, fell from rafters in neat arrangements like silken drapes.

"We make them ourselves," Mr. Hanohano said as we rested in the twilight on the simple stylized bridges. "We are fishermen in this family. All the menfolk are fishermen. My son-in-law, his brothers, my grandson, my father before me, my uncles, and those of our ohana who came before them."

The old man's voice had a musical lilt. The shed was like a small country chapel, and he, like a rector giving a tour. Fishing poles, rolls of varying weights of tackle, canoe oars, spears, and an assortment of glass-bottom squidding boxes were hung in neat arrangements among the nets. My father had spoken of the great fishing skills of Hawaiians.

"Do you still go out with the crew?" I asked.

"Not always. I haven't the stamina anymore. I don't like to sit in the canoe as a spectator."

"Where did you go to school?" I asked.

"Over fifteen years at Lahainaluna. After that I lived with a missionary family at Kohala for almost four years. I was a teacher there. Then I came back home to this valley to head the little school we have here."

"You were born here?"

"Many years ago! King Kalakaua had just been elected King. My own family were for Queen Emma. Do you know about this?"

"My great-grandparents lived across from her foster father's house on Nuuanu Street."

"They were both half-whites, like the Queen."

There was the much-lamented death of Emma's child, the Prince of Hawaii, at the age of five. Puna! There was no connection between Puna and the royal child.

"Did you like going to school at Lahainaluna?" I asked.

"Oh yes, very much! But I couldn't wait to get back home every time there was a holiday. My father was very good about letting me come home during those times. And all summer long I would fish to my heart's content until I got as black as a popolo berry by the time it was necessary to return to school." Certain of the old man's gestures and tones seemed familiar. "This house is built on stilts. We all sit on top of water here in Waipio. That's why so much taro is grown here. The water under us is full of o'opu. You know what o'opu is?"

"We catch them in the streams at home."

"Here all we have to do is bait our small hooks and let them down over the railing. Ah! Before you know it, we catch enough o'opu for a good feed. We cook them in the coals wrapped in ti leaf."

"Lawalu."

"Pololei kela!" The man's glossy eyes brightened. "You speak Hawaiian? I thought you came from the haole side of Ben's family."

"There is no haole side," I said. "Did you know Ben's mother?"

"I knew her well, and the one before her! Your uncle's last wife, Miriam, was my niece."

The old man was an older family-edition of Julian.

"If you will excuse me, my boy, I'll go see when the men are expected, or if they're coming home tonight at all! We say evening prayers in this family, and I'm the one who usually conducts them."

I loitered on the elevated walkway in the dusk.

Voices of women sounded somewhere and occasionally a dog's bark. The laughter of unseen children rolled in waves over the evening's stillness. I said Puna's name out loud. I had promised myself not to dwell on things. I let my eyes wander. There was much to please them.

A group of men in two canoes rowed upstream toward the house. They pulled in under the shed containing the fishing gear and then into a similar building next to it, where they hoisted the heavy canoes onto a board framework and rested them bottomside up. I slipped away before they finished and went to the main house. Ben had not returned from his gift-giving. I retired to the bedroom we had been given. In a short time Mr. Hanohano appeared.

"I'm going for my evening dip with my grandson and his wife. We bathe in the spring next to the watercress patch. Come and join us—it will refresh you. After that, we'll come back for evening prayers and have supper."

The old man told us a water spirit lived in the deliciously cold spring waters and occasionally revealed herself by shaping the long strands of algae into the form of a handsome young woman. The bride of a few months squealed with delighted fright. Her young husband would disappear below the surface and grab her feet or pinch her buttocks. I was surprised to hear them address each other as "Mommy" and "Daddy," but, as we bathed, I recognized their dreamy quality. I thought of the Dinwiddie twins and the mass of great-aunts and cousins who surrounded them. How different was their world! As we returned in the dark along a path that led through clumps of giant bamboo, the young Johnsons raced ahead like vigorous young phantoms in the hour for spirits.

"Hear the squeaks of the bamboo?" the old man chuckled. "It makes people think up all sorts of things. The Chinese call it the conversation of the spirits."

"Why does everbody on this island believe in spooks?"

One of his hands was on my shoulder. He squeezed it. "People don't *believe* in spirits here, Sonny. They *live* with them. They're a part of life!" He gave my back a gentle slap. "The wash house is right up here. Go and wash off and change, my boy. After that we will pray, and then eat. I'm sure the folks are ready by now."

We sat down to dine on the floor of a verandah lighted by lanterns. When I asked where Ben was and when he was expected back, theatrical questioning glances flashed among the members of the family. Mr. Hanohano, wearing now a pajama top and a clean dry pair of shorts, sat at one end of the verandah, his son-in-law, Kupihea Johnson, at the other. There were four other couples, including the youthful "Mommy" and "Daddy"; young Johnson's parents; his uncle and aunt; and a cousin and her husband, a lightly bearded Filipino, Crispin de La Cruz, who was a master fisherman with the long-handled spear. The children had been fed earlier and were now asleep in their own little house joined to the main one by an elevated boardwalk.

The old patriarch chanted a long Hawaiian prayer in melodious falsetto tones. I could not follow all he said, but my spirit seemed transported back hundreds of years.

Large bowls of poi sat in the middle of the area covered with lau'ae fern, and around them were numerous smaller dishes filled with raw, dark opai shrimp gathered fresh in the stream above the taro patches and prepared with ina mona and the unfurled leaves of the hoi'o fern. There were bowls of fish, beef stew, and salted beef cooked with taro leaves.

"Eat, boy, eat!" young Johnson insisted unnecessarily.

"Tasty, indeed, is the food of the land!" Mr. Hanohano said, eliciting a chorus of agreement from the family.

After supper, the old man disappeared. Two of the couples played cards for a while after clearing up. The older Johnson worked on what appeared to be an account book. His wife sewed together pieces of orange and yellow cloth to be appliqued to a kapa top in a design I had not seen before called Queen Kapiolani's comb. Crispin settled down in the storeroom to mend nets by lantern light. His wife sat near him and chattered and laughed about the day's fishing.

I went idly from one group to another before going to my room. I found a copy of the Bible and opened it to Exodus. It was like Hawaii. The impassioned rivalry between Moses and the Pharaoh. The powers of unseen forces at work everywhere. The pestilence. The rod turned into a snake. The frogs! There were so many croaking in the valley's taro patches. I fell asleep reading.

Late that night I awoke, and the heightened croaking of the frogs kept me from going back to sleep. Ben had not returned. I wandered outside and stood looking down at the shimmering water flowing quietly under the maze of stilts in the light of a three-quarter moon. Somewhere dogs were barking, audible during the diminuendos of frogs. Pharaoh's frogs! Now and again I heard the calls of a night heron, the Auku'u, flying down from cliff side nesting places to prey, like Pharaoh's sacred Ibis.

I was struck with an immense feeling of loneliness, of helplessness, and yet I could not forget the kindness of members of this household with their gentle, independent, and orderly way of life. What would my parents be doing at this hour? Puna's image came with restless insistence. He was beside me. I gripped the railing, feeling chilled and numb. The night seemed ageless.

"You can't sleep, boy?"

The soft voice came from nowhere. I couldn't immediately associate it, but when I finally jerked around, I saw Mr. Hanohano.

"One is always restless in a strange place. One is sleepless at times under any circumstances. I am sleepless myself tonight. I heard you come onto my landing. There is my room. I like to be a little apart. I read late into the night. Some people are easily bothered if they are aware a lamp is burning in some part of the house. Come into my room. We can talk there without being overheard. That is, if you care to."

"Yes, I do," I whispered, and followed him down the ramp. I was shivering, my eyes were watery.

"You are frightened, Sonny. Don't be afraid. You are safe here."

The old man opened a door. The light illuminated us slightly. His face had an almost incandescent glow. His bare torso was shining.

The room was furnished with a *hikie'e*—a platform, built against the wall, covered by a thin mattress—a table and two straight chairs. Above the table were two shelves of books: among them the enduring works of writers, poets—Alfred Lord Tennyson, Sir Walter Scott, Dickens, James Fenimore Cooper—interspersed with books on theology, botany, chemistry, physics, and physiology. I saw David Malo's *Moolelo o Hawaii,* Alexander's *Brief History of the Hawaiian People,* King Kalakaua's and Oscar Daggett's *Myths and Legends of Hawaii,* and Queen Liliuokalani's book with its familiar orange-red cover and gilt title: *Hawaii's Story by Hawaii's Queen,* "The Queen's Book," as it was referred to at home.

Photographs were set on ledges and on the table. A withered maile and mokihana seed lei was draped over a large photograph of a finely dressed Hawaiian woman.

"She was my wife. She died a long time ago. We met at Kohala. I have remained unmarried since she died. Her name was Rose—Rose Hanohano. That is my name—Hanohano. Do you know what it means?"

"My mother told me. . ." I had forgotten.

"It refers to the old gentry. Not the highest alii, but the gentry. In a sense, a snobbish word. It means people of quality. Quality in the way the English use the word. Dickens, for instance." His gaze fell on the rows of books.

Usually Hawaiians reveal their love of books only after you have known them for a long time. To make such a word association was extraordinary.

"Sit down, boy, sit down! Be comfortable! Don't be nervous! This is your house—a little shack, but it's your house!"

"It's a fine room! I'd like one like it!"

The old man smiled. He was sitting now on the hikie'e, his back against the wall, his lopped-off pajama pants pulled above the calf because his legs were drawn up to his chest. His hair was tousled.

"Your cousin, Ben Andrews, is down here to consult one of our native experts."

"My uncle thinks someone is performing hoomana on Puna. It might even be anaana."

"You know about these things?" His voice lifted, betraying his calm facade.

"It's evil!" I blurted.

"It's evil for people to harm one another. I've seen it happen too many times to scoff! But I do not discredit the ways of our forefathers. There were many kahunas who were not conjurers."

"I know! The lapaau, the aumakua. . ."

"Your cousin's mission is useless. He has come to see old Puali because your uncle thinks someone is out to hana-ino the little boy. This is not true."

"I agree. Puna is lonely and sad."

"Who wouldn't be in that terrible house. Excuse

me, my boy, for talking like this. The place is unclean. It's full of bad mana!"

"People make these things the old Hawaiians believed in sound so mysterious and frightening! They never say exactly why."

"Mana is spirit. It's the life force—unseen and without form. Mana is in people, in things. It's the essence of the universe. Good mana can be won by people who learn to do things skillfully—to do them well! A great expert has mana—like the kahunas of old who were correctly taught in their fields. They had real mana—not like the charlatans around today who only know how to scare people."

"Why do people say there's mana in rocks, in trees?"

"Rocks are powerful! They are strong in their silence. They endure. So do trees. Look at them! Be silent in your heart when you do. They will speak to you."

I loved rocks and trees. I always looked at them with awe.

"Do you think rocks have life?"

"Au'we," the old man responded with a gentle chortle. "Of course they do. They are not objects of flesh and blood, but they are alive in their own way."

"Do you know Laura Punohu?"

Mr. Hanohano chuckled, his head nodding up and down. "That's a very funny family," he said, dismissing the subject.

"You read a lot," I said, looking at his books.

"I used to. My eyes are no longer able to guide me through too many pages during an evening."

"I like to read everything!"

"Ah, my boy, you are one of those unfortunate people destined to be a man of learning. Knowledge is confounding."

The old schoolteacher launched into island history, ancient customs, and the change that came in the nineteenth century: "our people, our history." He spoke of dead chiefs, dead kings and queens, their triumphs and tribulations, as though all the complex welter of their times, their acts and beliefs were current events. Had I visited Puu Kohala? It was only a step from the harbor at Kawaihae. One of the great heiau of old. Mr. Hanohano brought out a scrapbook of clippings of Samuel Kamakau's historical writings from nineteenth-century Hawaiian language newspapers.

"Not enough has been written about our people. Not enough that pictures things from the point of view of the Hawaiians. Malo and Kamakau are only a beginning. Our ways, our feelings, need interpretation. But who's to do the job? This is the sad fact. There are fewer and fewer of our people who know the language, who have the training, who have the *iki*—the inclination and understanding."

I was under the spell of the old man's words, the rise and fall of his voice, the dramatic changes of expression that turned his squarish bony face into masks of joy one moment, chagrin the next, anger, exuberance, worry; the quizzical look which means, do you see? do you understand? "Maopopo oe keia? Maopopo oe kela?"

The scrapbook was put back into place.

"Your young cousin Puna is going to die."

The silence was blank.

Old Hanohano looked at me with eyes that pleaded understanding, but seemed red and burning with rage. "Do not ask how I know this, but I do!" His voice rasped as though he were struck by great fatigue, as though he were dying. "Maopopo oe keia?"

"What are you?" I choked. "A Goddamned kahuna? How dare you say this?"

Finally the old man said gently, "Let us go and walk on the beach. The dawn will be breaking soon. It will cleanse us. We will pray to Lono. Let's go and greet the new day from the seashore."

I followed him on the ashy sands of Waipio Beach.

He recited fragments of old chants. "These are good prayers. Prayers to Lono. I say them for you—for your future. Don't be afraid, my boy, don't be afraid."

Violent waves rolled in from the reef and crashed on the black sand. Dark clouds raced across the Waimanu cliffs toward Hiilawe. The first pale yellow began to streak the horizon. I could not read the signs of the coming weather as they appeared in massive cloud formations above the sea.

"The dawn is a rebirth. The dawn is the beginning—a time to rejoice—a time to show reverence—a time to link oneself with God."

His chanting roiled my fears and questions.

"These waters, these thundering waters! So clean! So powerful! Look at the light coming from the horizon! A new day, my boy a new day! Come, my boy, strip off your clothes. Let us bathe in these clean waters. Let us be enriched and cleansed by the powers of the sea!"

He unfastened the strings of his pajamas, stood naked with his arms wide open as though to embrace the full spread of the new day. He said something in Hawaiian and ran into the green wall of an oncoming wave. He disappeared for a few moments, and then I saw his brown body bobbing in the foamy waters. He looked like some sea-borne turtle. I stripped off my clothes and ran yelling like a savage into the pounding surf.

Joe arrived at noon to tell us that Puna had been killed by one of the goats Uncle Fred kept to feed his dogs. We set out with Mr. Hanohano to tell Ben, who was at the house of Ezekiel Puali about a mile from the Johnson compound.We walked along maze-like paths through ancient taro patches. Black and white Muscovy ducks and Peking whites abounded in and at the sides of the patches which were unplanted, but watery.

Puali's house sat in the middle of a yard surrounded by a red picket fence, towering mango and breadfruit trees, and thick hedges of the tallest green ti I had ever seen.

"The house of one of the masters of hanky-panky of our times," Mr. Hanohano said.

"Oiaio no," Joe grunted.

We entered the garden, a maelstrom of flowering annuals: marigolds, coxcomb, and bachelor buttons. The oblong house was painted the same red as the fence. A heavy, slightly bearded man sat on the wide verandah which ran across the front.

The exchange of greetings was coolly matter-of-fact. Old Puali was dressed in a pair of ragged dungarees and a snow-white undershirt. His hair and beard were stringy. His dark eyes seemed mad and fiercely penetrating.

"You have come with the bad news about the boy. I tried to tell the big one that last night. He would not believe me." Puali spoke in a deep singsong. "The prayers were not propitious. They went askew. I told the big fellow to refrain from eating and drinking. You know these Andrews—poʻo paʻakiki! Who is the handome young flower of the taro who has come with you?"

Mr. Hanohano explained.

"He is fairer than his cousin. He's from a different stalk of the breadfruit tree." Old Puali said slyly that Ben was asleep in a cottage behind the house, in the company of one of Puali's granddaughters. "They are entwined like an ie-ie vine embracing a giant koa tree." He laughed oddly. "Did you drink the waters of life from the well of that handsome young hapa-haole? You crafty old goat." Puali referred to an ancient ritual of an esoteric sect of kahuna performed in the initiation rites of certain young chiefs.

"You mock us," Mr. Hanohano said. "Be careful."

Joe grunted and scratched his neck.

"There is no mockery in what I say," Puali answered with irritation. He called out. A middle-aged woman came to the door. "Get that big hapa-haole. His family are here to take him home." The woman disappeared.

"So you unfolded your wisdom last night, you flabby old steer," Mr. Hanohano said.

"And what did you unfurl, schoolmaster? Your withered scrotum?"

"Pig!"

"Be careful in this garden what words you use, schoolmaster!"

"Pig!"

"The maggots are just as eager to eat out your liver, old man, as they are anyone else's! You are not immune!"

"Keep your rubbishy threats to yourself!"

"The ka'upu bird is calling! What is the food it is calling for?"

"For a man! For you!"

"Maggots take root in your stomach—disease festers in your groin. Maggots eat your diseased balls!"

Mr. Hanohano unbuttoned his trousers, pulled out his penis, and began to urinate. He caught the yellow liquid in his hand and rubbed it on his shoulders, over his torso, and on me. The next handful he flicked in the air around us. Joe pulled me back toward the gate.

"That will not protect you, you stubby prick, you!" Puali rose from his place, lunged for the railing, and began to shout things in Hawaiian I could not understand.

"Dizz eez tare-ble! Really tare-ble! But dat ole bag of shit on da porch no can evah beat Mr. Hanohano!"

Ben was in the doorway, disheveled, swaying. Joe went to the porch steps. Mr. Hanohano came to my side.

"Forgive me, child. Some of our ways are necessarily vulgar. I did that to protect us. This old devil has for years and years been trying to cast me under his spell. He would like to control everyone in this valley. He robs people of everything they have. Charges them exorbitant fees for his predictions and his ugly death-dealing prayers. He blasphemes the ways of our ancestors. We have always been bitter enemies. He has powers, I grant you, but he's not as effective as he likes to think he is. A charlatan, pure and simple."

I felt a grimness creep into me. My emotions hardened. Mr. Hanohano walked me outside of the yard to a nearby mango tree.

"Don't be afraid, Sonny. Don't let any of this touch you. It is all rubbish! The real things, the strong things, are the ones we talked about last night."

"I'm not afraid of anything!" I growled.

"Good! Good! Keiki lei aloha! You are a fine boy. You will do great things!" He embraced me with a gentle certainty. I sank my nose into his chest muscles and drank in the smell of the sea, clinging still to his silken skin. He pressed me closer as though to give me the strength of his mana. I pulled away. Memory of the early morning intimacy at the beach made me tremble.

"I want to go back to the house."

"Wait, boy! Ben is coming!"

I walked on.

The donkeys were readied for our departure. Joe had managed to get drunk. I dreaded to think of the drinking that must be taking place at Fred's house.

Mr. Hanohano pulled me to one side. "It's been a happy experience for me to meet you, Mark. More than I can say." He gripped my hand. His eyes were wet. "Too bad your visit has ended in such sadness. Life and death! They are always with us! Good-bye, my boy!" He embraced me tightly. Tears spilled over his bony cheeks. "Write to me, if you like. I will always remember our talks last night. Our walk along the beach to watch the dawn come in. Aloha keiki lei aloha! Aloha nui!" he said and walked away.

We made our way slowly up the green cliffs, those towering natural battlements that had guarded Waipio Valley from the world for so long.

My memory of the two day vigil before Puna was buried is as vague as some half-remembered dream. Images come in fragments—connected to sounds, to smells. The hum of hushed voices is disturbed by occasional outbursts of keening. Words are said—or chanted, really. The sources are brown faces—old and not so old, wrinkled and covered with moisture. There are eyes, dimmed and reddened with tears, eyes black and lustrous, eyes that love and hate and accuse. There are the choking, drugging smells of flowers.

Masses of flowers are banked round the white coffin, some fashioned into homemade wreaths and sprays on bamboo frames. The flowers are almost vulgar: too many, too prominent in color and fragrances. Helpful ladies, who show up quickly after the announcement of Puna's death, receive the floral offerings, carefully store accompanying cards in a calabash, and tax their ingenuity to place the flowers in such a way as to please mourners and givers alike. It is difficult in the growing clutter of the small brown parlor. There are sprays of baby's breath and forget-me-not; wreaths of fern, of maile and kukuna o kala: the unique flower-like bracts of mangrove blossoms colored orange, brown, and chartreuse. There are flower wreaths: carnations and roses, and a single heart-shaped piece fashioned from baroquely-colored pansies and maidenhair fern from the Punohu house next door. Running diagonally across the heart of flower faces is a lavender band on which *Darling Puna* has been satin-stitched in white silk thread. The furniture, the family portaits, the photographs, the glass case of neolithic oddments and the stuffed monkeys are obliterated by the masses of blooms. Ropes of roses drape the coffin as a flowery bier. Around its open hood, where the pale face and black hair of the dead boy lie in glossy folds of white satin, there are strands and strands of pikake and a few ilima leis from Kona. Over the body, two kahili are slowly and continuously waved to ward off evil essences and ease the boy's chiefly spirit into the next world.

All Waimea has come during the two-day wake to pay last respects to Puna. The numbers seem to exceed those who attended the dance at the Ellen Kiliwehi Stevenson Hall or Puna's birthday luau. Mourners come from as far away as Hilo and Ka'u. Others have come up from Kona, and some from Kohala. A multitude of ohana show up. "My God," Fred has said at some point in the proceedings, "all the relatives of all my dead wives have come." These are mostly Hawaiian families with large broods of children: the girls dressed in white, the boys in blue serge trousers and white shirts and black bow ties.

The strings of people continue: old mama sans and their wrinkled farmer husbands, Chinese store-keepers, and the taro farmers of Waipio, haoles from sugar plantations, Portuguese from their small ranches along the Hamakua Coast. Fred greets them all, his face pale as the midnight sky in the moonlight. "My cousin's boy," he says, pointing to me. The callers seem satisfied, some even happy to learn this unimportant fact. I am at Fred's side most of the time, near the white coffin. He is loath to have me leave him. When I do and am gone too long, he sends for me. He takes my hand. "Stay, Markie! Stay with me!"

The house creaks and groans with people. Some have stayed for two days and nights, sleeping as they can in chairs, in corners or in the spare bedrooms. Offerings of food and okolehao flow into the house. Shifts of helpers prepare coffee and rolls, sandwiches and cake for the mourners. These are varied with servings of soft fried noodles, nishi me and sushi, and Chinese roast pork, as offerings pile up in the kitchen and pantry.

Uncle Palani's suite, including my room, has been converted into a cloak room. Chinese shawls, coats and jackets, a shower of hats of all kinds—the men's banded with leis of feathers or flowers, or both—weigh down the great four-poster. Those with less grief to show, who want to gossip and carry on, retreat into these rooms and the porch after they have stuffed themselves in the kitchen or breakfast room.

The odor of flowers. I feel sickened. The closeness of the air in the brown wallpapered parlor makes me hoʻopailua. Henry and Leihulu fidget nearby, shedding hot tears each time there is an outburst of grief-showing among the mourners.

There is soft sweet music. Paniolos and their wives form groups to sing the old meles of Waimea or hymns. I grip the arm of the Belter sofa as a group sings *Nearer My God to Thee*. A young woman with a beautiful voice sings *Rock of Ages*. I want to run from the room. Fred grips my arm. The tears flow down. The crying is shameless. It is going on everywhere. Those who come into the house shed tears at the first sight of the dead boy. I avoid looking at his still, gray face.

A huge wreath of cattleya orchids and Boston

fern rests near the coffin. It has come from the chatelaines and paniolos of the Pittman Ranch. A great spray of white butterfly orchids arrives by sampan taxi, sent by Aunt Hannah Shipley and her son Gresham. The taxi unloads a new wave of mourners. My father's telegram is delivered. The message from my parents is in Hawaiian. "Our hearts are breaking with yours. Our thoughts, our love is with you all. With profound sadness." Fred grips me around the shoulders. "Oh Markie! Oh Markie!" he wails.

It is Saturday night. Puna will be buried in the morning. The parlor is stilled and, for some reason, nearly empty of mourners. Someone has taken Fred off to feed him. He has touched no food for two days. He goes reluctantly, Lepeka enjoining him vehemently to "eat something for you strenth's sake. It help you beah up, Analu."

A very old couple stand over the coffin and say things I cannot understand, imitating the speech of small children. They run wrinkled fingers over the boy's face, his forehead. They join me at the sofa.

"I am Miriam Lono's grandaunt," the ancient woman says. "This is my husband, Solomon Kekipi. We have come from Hilo."

I greet them dispiritedly. I am exhausted. My eyes are swollen. "I am Analu's cousin from Honolulu."

"On the father's side?" the old man asks.

"Ae. Analu e hoahanau o papa iau."

I am weary of people's surprise at my little Hawaiian.

There is a desolate cry outside the front door. It is a kuwo cry: the cry of grief as someone arrives from afar, chanting expressions of aloha for the dead. The front doors open wide. It is Julian. He is dressed in a black suit, a white shirt and black string tie. He rushes into the room; quavering chanted words of lament gush from his mouth. His string tie is loose; it dangles from his collar. At the coffin he buries his face in the folds of white satin. Flower leis lie tangled about his head. His body shakes as he lifts his fists and gently pounds the edges of the casket.

"Keiki! Keiki!" he wails. "Child of my heart's love! My most precious flower! Fruit of my sister's womb! Why do you leave us this way? Keaha! Keaha! Why, why break our hearts? Take mine! Take me! What have I done? What? Tell me, love's child, tell me why!" His cries are like nothing I have ever heard. His wailing seems to punish everyone in sight. They bend their heads. Julian's grief is too much to absorb. I want him to leave.

"His heart is broken," the old woman says.

"How heavy is the grief of Kauikeaouli," her husband replies, using the proverbial expression of the young king's mourning for his sister, joined to him in the last-known pio marriage of the mana-rank chiefs.

"Keaha! Keaha!" Julian cries in torment.

Fred was at the parlor door, Lepeka near him.

I dash from the Belter sofa. "Please, Uncle Fred, don't send him away!"

"He is a murderer!" he mutters.

Ben and Hanford take their father away. I return to the sofa. The room is filled with people. Julian comes to me, falls on his knees, buries his head in my lap.

"Why, Markie? Why dis happen to my Puna?"

I cannot speak. I stroke Julian's thick hair, glossy and slippery with Tres Flores brilliantine.

"Why, Markie? You a smaht boy, tell me why!" He pleads with deep animal sobs. He grips my shoulders and shakes me painfully.

Joe and two cowboys come into the room and take Julian away. He does not resist. His sobbing continues, but the grief that was lodged in the naau, the guts, is spent. His black-suited form escapes quietly through the front doors—as limp as a shadow.

I take the old lady's bony hand. "Your grand-nephew, tutu? Puna's uncle." I can no longer hold back the tears. They gush and flow wantonly over my face.

The air was sweet with the odors of eucalyptus and cypress held captive in the morning dew. Joe and I were driving to Kawaihae where I would board the *Kamoi* for Honolulu. The narrow road from Kamuela village cut in sweeping curves through the open lava wastes to the hot bay far below the mists of Waimea. Our few words were in Hawaiian. We passed kiawe trees and the ruins of the Puu Kohala temple. Joe unloaded my bags and boxes packed with smoked beef and pork. One box contained pheasant skins for feather leis, Fred's gift to my father.

"There'll be a delay until the cattle are loaded," the clerk told me. "The sharks are giving us trouble. They already tore hell outa one of the steers. But don't go too far from the wharf."

The *Kamoi* sat calmly in the translucent water. A group of fishermen in a canoe were splashing with their paddles to drive away the sharks. One man was in the water.

"Damn fool Hawaiian!" Joe spat.

We shook hands, and he walked in his funny bouncy way back to the old Packard.

The cowboys roped a steer and raced it out of the corral into the sea.

"They're making another try." It was Mrs. Charles K. L. White, dressed in a spotless white silk shirtwaist dress and brown and white spectator pumps. She spoke with a clipped Boston accent.

Zachary, her younger son, was a classmate of mine. "Hi, Mark! I almost didn't recognize you. You got skinny this summer! You've grown a lot taller!"

Mrs. White scanned me thoroughly, disapproving of my cowboy clothes.

"I'm going away to Choate," Zachary went on. "Char-Boy is going to Princeton."

The bored elder brother resembled Daniel Keaka, their nineteenth-century great-grandfather, a lesser chief but one of unquestioned ability. He had adjusted to his time, had been granted substantial landholdings, and left his family enormously rich.

The boys were dressed alike in gray flannels, white buckskin shoes, and ivory-colored blazers. A Japanese maid in kimono fluttered about them, making dainty but meaningless adjustments to their clothing.

"Did you see the twins at Waimea?" Mrs. White asked.

"Some of these sharks," Zachary interrupted, "live in underwater caves near my uncle's fish ponds. They always feed in Kawaihae Bay. We used to watch them coming home. Every evening on the dot, at sunset!"

"Now, Zach, don't exaggerate," said his mother, sharply.

I turned away and walked to the corral, where the cowboys were preparing to take another group of steers into the water. If the sharks didn't get them, they would be delivered to the slaughterhouse in Kalihi. There was still time to see the ruins of the Puu Kohala heiau I had been told so much about.

I took a well-trodden trail through thickets of kolu bushes and haole koa. The land rose sharply from the seashore to the top of a puu, or promontory, on which the great heiau was constructed. On the slope, I met the high walls of a smaller heiau, Mailikini, where commoners—soldiers and artisans—worshipped in times of war. The enclosure was narrow, about two hundred feet long, and rather unimpressive. I had an excellent view of the bay, but didn't look long for fear of seeing the sharks in the clear water.

Higher, the hillside was clear of brush. A few kiawe trees shaded the rocky slopes. Wild ilima bushes were heavily in bloom, their pale orange flowers bursting like tiny flames against the gray-green foliage. I reached the first group of steps leading to the heiau entrance. I stopped, looked hard at the reddish rocks of the base wall, and then turned around toward the ocean. I could see the entire bay below. I could make out the fencing of the corral through the lattice of kiawe branches. The little ship was a black blob in the open expanse of cerulean waters. The sharks were swimming in large circles around the canoe. To the left of me were the fog-shrouded summits of Mauna Loa and Hualalai; to the right, the wide, dry, scarred stretch leading to the foothills of the Kohala mountains. In the mid-morning light, the whipped white froth along the ragged coastline of black rock, the blues and greens of the ocean, were all brilliantly clear and appeared very close. The man was still in the water, swimming near the canoe.

I turned back to the ancient rock steps leading to the interior of Puu Kohala. A stony path, intersected at points by two or three further steps, led along the side of the wall facing the sea. A small opening at the corner led up into the temple enclosure. At one end, raised about four feet above the temple floor, was a platform paved with large round flat-topped river stones. I chose one at the end and sat down. The sun was hot and still, and there was no shade. From somewhere came the sound of an old person chanting.

I saw the launch making its way toward the ship with the heads of six fat Stevenson steers roped securely to the sides and jutting above the water. The launch made its way slowly into the deeper waters of the bay. The three men in the launch stood watch, holding oars, and scanning the water for sharks. A black fin cut the water as clean as a surfboard and as fast. The men gestured wildly and splashed their oars. Their cries were barely audible. The man in the water started swimming toward the shore. Near the launch, the water reddened. A dozen black fins raced across the bay. I turned away, trembling.

"You are sitting where only the chiefs are allowed. It is for those of Keawe to sit on these stones." An old man in torn dungarees and a white shirt frayed at the sleeves was standing above me. He wore a red handkerchief around his withered neck. A stringy white beard dangled like dried grass from his chin. His eyes were tiny and chocolate brown. "I am the kahu of this place. You are sitting on the chiefs' stones. Even if you are a haole and don't understand, you should not sit there."

"I come from chiefs," I said in Hawaiian.

The old man wheezed, choked, coughed profusely, and spat several times. "You are hapa-haole! Forgive me, keiki! And what are the names of your grandmothers?" I gave him the full names, each fifteen to twenty-five letters long. He questioned me closely, plundering his memory for oddments. Then he began to chant.

"Do you understand this?" he asked. "I am chanting your family genealogy—one branch."

"I am honored."

"For centuries my ancestors have been the kahunas of this place. My great-grandfather was a priest here in the time of the Great One, the Lonely One, Kamehameha. There was great power here. The gods gave this power to Kamehameha, though the temple is more ancient than he."

"He sacrificed Keoua Kuahuula here."

A shout reached us from the bay.

"The sharks are at their play," said the old man. "They are being whimsical."

"They're beasts! They tore a steer to shreds!"

"A small sacrifice from such a rich source! The sharks have always lived in the bay. When the steers are loaded, it annoys the guardians."

"They're destructive!"

"To some, they are loving and mindful. They protect those who are theirs. My great-grandson often swam in the water talking to them, warning them to go away before the infidels could bring out their rifles and dynamite. I have been praying here for the same reason. When the sharks are angered they seek revenge. They hunger for the flesh of man." The old man looked toward the bay. "The Great One used to fight the shark in these waters. There is a stone down there. Come to the edge. I will show you."

"I don't want to see those things eating the steer."

"He has already been devoured. Their bellies are full. They have gone to loll in their caves under the reef."

We walked slowly to the edge of the lower temple floor.

"There was his stone, the stone of Kamehameha, under those kiawe trees. He sat there and waited until the priest from Puu Kohala told him of the right moment to plunge into the sea and go after the shark that his warriors had driven into the waters close to the shore. There were no trees on this hillside in those days. It was open to the gods. The Great One ran down the hill and into the waters where he met the shark head on. The shark had the name of Keoua Kuahuula, one of his most hated enemies. In the heat of anger, the Great One stunned the shark with blows, opened its jaws and tore them asunder until the shore was red with the blood of the enemy." The ancient's voice had worked up to a high, reedy pitch. He chanted his last words: "What a thing to have been privileged to see! Only the gods can grant the strength given to the Lonely One. My grandfathers witnessed the strength of the Great Kamehameha!"

"The strength," I said, "which killed and sacrificed Keoua Kuahuula!"

The old one smiled and said: "In the olden days the gods hungered for the blood of man. I did not see this happen. My grandfathers did. When I was born this temple was in ruins."

In the silence, someone was calling me from below. A man was climbing toward Mailikini, waving at me to come down. I started for the stone steps leading out of the heiau.

"Stay!"

"I must go to Honolulu!"

The ancient red eyes penetrated me. "You will be a guest in my home. I will tell you wonderful things about this place, about all the great ones of the past. I will give you the history of Puu Kohala. Stay!" he commanded.

As I back away from the old man, chiefs are gathering in the brilliant noonday sun. Attendants carry kahili, tabu sticks, and images held aloft on long poles. The walls of the heiau teem with wooden sculptures of angry, protective deities. The oracle tower, covered with white tapa, rises fifty feet from the lower platform. Under the tower, kahunas in white tapa, stand chanting prayers.

The chiefs take their seats on the row of stones along the edge of the higher platform. They wear crested feather helmets and large-patterned cloaks of red and yellow feathers. The Great One arrives. His helmet and cloak are a purity of rarest yellow feathers. He sits. Drums beat. A chant is intoned—vibrant, vehement. The chiefs sit immobile, and the scene dissolves into its own eternity. The old man and I are alone. Someone is calling my name.

"Stay, child! Stay! You belong to us." The old man whines, pawing me, holding my sleeve. With a seizure of strength, I pull away and run pell-mell down the hillside.

Design and typesetting by ParaGraphics, Inc., Bloomfield, NJ

Printing and binding by Thomson-Shore, Inc., Dexter, MI